Queens of Iris

Queens of Iris

Seasons of the Veil - Book Zero

Written by Aaron McQueen

Illustrations by Jennifer Lange
Edited by Hannah Bormann

Book Zero of the Seasons of the Veil series by Aaron McQueen

Copyright © 2020 Aaron McQueen and McQueen Serial Fantasy

All rights reserved

ISBN: 978-1-7343646-2-0

This book is a work of fiction. Any resemblance to actual events, locations, or persons, living or dead, is entirely coincidental.

For Theresa

A Strange Land

The spell began and ended with a flash of light. The ground leapt up at Gwynedd in a rush. Her palms scraped against the ground and she rolled across leaf-strewn dirt, grunting as she slid to a violent stop. Jumping to her feet, her eyes darted around, scanning the scene. The Foxglove was missing.

The marble walls of the high chamber and the sounds of the battle were similarly absent. Gwynedd found herself on a deserted road in the middle of a dense forest, surrounded only by calm wind, the twitter of birds, and the soft click of insects. The road stretched out on either side, sloping gently down until it passed out of sight. Above, the sky unfolded in a field of endless blue, and the brush beside the path grew thick with strange flowers and fruit.

Where am I? she thought. *And where is Bronwyn?*

An explosion of light burst into the air and her friend came tumbling down, striking the earth with a hard thump.

"Oof!" she grunted, rolling into a crouch. She glanced up at Gwynedd, and her eyes shot around the road. Her hand flew to the hilt of her sword, and she said, "What the hell was that? Gwynedd, are you alright?"

"I'm fine," Gwynedd replied, pulling her up.

Bronwyn dusted herself off and looked around. "Where are we?"

Gwynedd's eyes returned to the trees. "I have no idea. Where is the Foxglove? Did you see it?"

"It was right in front of us. What happened?"

"I'm not sure. Where are the others?"

Bronwyn straightened her heavy green cloak, shedding a layer of dirt and leaves. "I don't know. Omnibor was with us. Last I heard, Parah was in the rotunda, trying to hold the corridor, and Fionn was heading for the vault to reinforce the lower breach."

"And the dryads?"

"Outside, gods help them. The palace is completely surrounded. What are we doing here?"

"Something must have gone wrong with the spell," Gwynedd answered. "We have to get back. The Foxglove must be around here. Help me look."

Bronwyn began walking in a circle, eyes on the ground. Gwynedd did the same, mind racing. Had she miscalculated? The weapon should not have taken them anywhere.

"Here!" Bronwyn called.

Gwynedd ran over and threw herself to the ground, where Bronwyn was brushing handfuls of leaves off a pile of dirt. Gwynedd took her stone knife out of her belt dug, until the earth revealed the fine grain of the Foxglove's wooden face. It's eyes lay shut, and its mouth, closed. Copper hair fell solid over its shoulders, green with age, partly concealing the statue's delicately carved features, fashioned from polished wood and inlaid with glimmering rivulets of gemstone, metal, and milky white rock.

"It looks asleep," Bronwyn said. "And look at its hair. How long has it been lying here?"

"It can't have been more than a few minutes," Gwynedd said.

Bronwyn brushed the last of the leaves away. The Foxglove was buried up to its waist. "Well, it certainly doesn't look it."

"It doesn't matter," said Gwynedd. "We'll wake it up and go back to the palace. There's still time."

She ran her fingers across the creature's smooth features, opening her mind to the construct as she invited its huge consciousness in, but the Foxglove's closed eyes remained impassively shut, arms folded over its stomach in still and silent repose.

"It's not working," Gwynedd said, gritting her teeth as her fingers pressed harder and harder against the wood. "The magic won't come."

Bronwyn leaned down. "Why not?"

"There's no connection," Gwynedd replied, sitting back on her heels. "Either I can't find it, or the construct is fighting me."

Bronwyn pulled the Foxglove out of the dirt. Crumbling lumps of soil and pebbles scattered off its body as she dragged it to a gentle slope beside the road. "Why would it resist?"

"No reason I can think of," Gwynedd said, joining her.

"Want me to try?"

Gwynedd raised an eyebrow. "You? You're not a practitioner, or even an apprentice."

"Hey, the world needs warriors too."

"Not today," Gwynedd said, laying her hands again on the Foxglove's shoulders. She shut her eyes and tried again. A few minutes passed uneventfully before she gave up a second time. Sitting back on her heels, she sighed and said, "Nothing."

Bronwyn scratched her scalp beneath the long curls of her hair. She puffed out an exhausted breath. "Blazes, it's hot out here. I'll die from sweating. Do you have any water left?"

"None," Gwynedd said. "Just my knife and a few coins."

"I've only got my sword, some rope, and half a biscuit. Why won't your magic work?"

Gwynedd gathered a clump of flowers in her fist and pulled them up. The tiny yellow blossoms were unfamiliar. "Maybe it's this place," she said. "You've traveled more of Iris than I have. Do you know this forest?"

Bronwyn surveyed the road and the woods. "I'm not sure. Maybe somewhere to the east, but it would have to be past the Volglade."

"That's a long way."

"It's the only place I've never been."

Gwynedd scrunched up her cheek in puzzlement. "Why would the Foxglove send us all the way out here? And alone?"

"Don't ask me. It's your invention."

"Our invention," Gwynedd insisted.

"Nonsense. It's night folk magic."

"True, but without the help of the other races, creating it would have been impossible. We can all take credit, such as it is."

Bronwyn scraped her boot across the ground, glancing back and forth along the desolate road. "I guess we should get moving then," she said. "Maybe we can find someone to help us."

Gwynedd shut her eyes and opened her mind, inviting the world in, hoping for a glimpse of the surrounding countryside. No images came, nor any impressions of any kind. "I've got nothing," she said.

"Then we should head downhill. Better chance of finding water and a settlement," said Bronwyn, pointing. "That way."

Gwynedd grabbed the Foxglove by the shoulders. "Help me tip it on its feet, and give me your rope."

"You're going to carry it?"

"One of us has to. We can't leave it behind."

Bronwyn untied a rope from her hip and lashed it around the Foxglove, tying a makeshift harness. "I'll carry it," she said. The dense muscle of her arms flexed as she hefted the construct up onto her back.

"Thank the gods," said Gwynedd, wiping her forehead with her sleeve. "I was hoping you'd say that."

Bronwyn rolled her eyes. "You've gotten soft, old friend. You should spend more time outdoors."

They marched downhill, boots crunching against hard earth, following the road as they baked in the midday heat. Gwynedd giggled as Bronwyn's ample hair became a mass of brown tangles and sweat.

"Laugh it up," Bronwyn said. "Gods, why is it so hot? Isn't it supposed to be fall?"

Gwynedd looked up at the trees, heavy with summer blossoms and fruit. "At least you're day folk. You'll tan."

Bronwyn adjusted the ropes over her shoulders and looked up at the sky. "I can't see the horizon. Maybe the Foxglove moved us somewhere to the north. It's summer there this time of year."

"It doesn't make any sense," Gwynedd replied.

"Hopefully we'll get some answers soon. Somebody built this road, so there must be people. We just have to find them."

A Most Peculiar Folk

Bronwyn's shoulders strained as the walk grew longer. The weight of the Foxglove hung like a fallen log, and the heat of the day swirled around them like desert wind. Nearly an hour had passed, and they hadn't come across any sign of anyone, or even a single drop of water. Her mouth felt as though she'd stuffed it with cotton, and her throat stung dry as it burned.

She glanced over at Gwynedd. Her friend wasn't a frail woman, but the night folk were a thin, pale people, fair folk of the moon and the twilight. Her skin would burn if the forest gave way to open country, and Bronwyn could already see her dark eyes watering. Nevertheless, as a queen, she was beautiful, tall and thin as her arms drew slender lines from her shoulders to her waist, far more delicate than Bronwyn's own day folk frame. The midnight blue of her robes—which she had undone—caught the noon light and glimmered with subtle hues of indigo and purple.

"Anything yet?" Gwynedd asked.

Gwynedd probably couldn't see more than a dozen feet in front of them. Bronwyn turned back to the road and said, "Nothing. How are you feeling?"

"Fantastic," her friend replied, rubbing her eyes. She swept a hand back through her close-cropped hair, sending a spattering of sweat out behind her head. "Gods, I wish we had some water."

"Agreed," said Bronwyn.

The heels of the Foxglove dragged along the road behind them, leaving twin ruts in the dirt.

"Wasn't this thing supposed to destroy the enemy?" Bronwyn asked, glancing back at its stiff wooden form.

"It should have," Gwynedd answered. "I don't know what happened. The Foxglove is connected to every element of nature. It has more than enough power to do whatever we could possibly want."

Bronwyn gave a sad chuckle. "A hundred years to build a weapon, and it turns out to be a dud."

"I'm sure we can fix it if we can get our magic working again. Let's just hope whatever's stopping it doesn't extend beyond the forest."

"You think it's the trees?" said Bronwyn.

"Or the flowers. I've studied herb lore all my life, and I've never seen anything like them. There's no telling what properties they might have."

Bronwyn glanced toward the roadside. The little yellow blooms practically covered the ground, cropping up like weeds between every blade of grass. In the trees, little brown birds, flashing with smears of red, white, and yellow, flitted through the branches, their appearances as strange and alien as figures in a children's book.

"We must be a long way from home," she said.

Gwynedd gave her shoulder a reassuring squeeze. "Don't worry," she replied. "I'll get us back."

The sound of a creaking wood stirred behind them. For a moment, Bronwyn thought the Foxglove might have stirred awake, but as she looked back, she saw a wooden cart coming up the trail, drawn by a pair of huge, hoofed beasts she couldn't identify.

"Someone's coming," she said. "Behind us."

Gwynedd stopped and turned, shouting. "Hey!"

There was no reply.

"Can you help us!" Gwynedd called.

The cart approached at a languid pace, barely faster than the speed at which they'd been walking. As it drew near, Gwynedd squinted and her eyes went wide.

"What is that?!"

Bronwyn looked up at the driver, perched on a wooden bench atop the cart. It was a man, rugged-looking and dirty. His broad shoulders and knotted muscles gave him the look of a dwarf, but his eyes were bright and round like a gnome's, and he was tall. Were he on his feet, he could look a night folk woman in the eye, and there were no taller people among the six races.

"I have no idea," she said. "Could it be another race?"

"Another race?" Gwynedd said. "And we've never heard of them? Not likely, and what about these animals?"

"I don't care," said Bronwyn. "Maybe he can give us a ride."

She lugged the Foxglove out into the path of the cart. "Hello? Sir? Can you help us?"

The man didn't answer.

"Sir!" she said again, raising her voice. She reached out to catch him by the ankle as he passed.

Her fingers dispersed into a fine mist and passed through his body.

"What in blazes!" she exclaimed, yanking her hand away. She staggered back and lost her balance, falling down to the side of the road with a grunt. She stared at her hand in shock as her digits reformed.

"Hey! Watch where you're going!" Gwynedd snapped, pounding her fist against the cart is it carried on. The wood answered her anger with a soft thump, and she ran over to Bronwyn. "Are you all right?"

"Did you see that?" Bronwyn said, still staring at her hand. She massaged it with her thumb, double-checking its firmness.

"I did. Something is very wrong here."

A dreadful thought occurred to Bronwyn in that moment. "Could we be dead?"

Gwynedd frowned. "I've never heard any stories like this, and I don't think we'd be thirsty if we were dead. Maybe the man is some kind of illusion."

"And the cart is driving itself? And besides, wouldn't the illusion go all…" She waggled her hand back and forth.

"Your guess is as good as mine," Gwynedd said. "At least we know we're going in the right direction."

"And how do we know that?" Bronwyn asked.

"That man has to be going somewhere."

Bronwyn took a deep breath and let it out in a ragged sigh. "Right, right. At least we know that."

Reaching down, she picked the Foxglove back up and they resumed walking, following the cart from a safe distance. Huge bags of grain filled the open carriage behind the driver's bench.

"You know," Gwynedd said, "the man might be enchanted in some way, but the cart felt normal enough. We could try climbing on the back. Those sacks look awfully comfortable, and in another few miles, I'm bound to collapse."

Bronwyn narrowed her eyes at the cart and the man, flexing her fingers. "You may have a point. That guy is lucky I can't touch him; I'd pummel him in the face."

Gwynedd jogged up behind the cart and planted her hands on the open back. The boards held her, and she hopped up. With a grunt, Bronwyn tossed the Foxglove in beside her and climbed aboard.

"How come that guy doesn't say something?" she said.

"He must not be able to hear us," Gwynedd replied.

Bronwyn lay down and rocked her shoulders back and forth, easing herself in between the grain sacks and groaning as she felt her muscles relax. "At least we're done walking, and I don't have to carry that damned statue anymore."

The trees began to thin as they neared the edge of the forest, and Gwynedd glanced forward apprehensively. "Can you see if there's a blanket?" she said.

Bronwyn furrowed her brow. "You're cold?"

"For shade."

"Ah," Bronwyn said, turning to crawl forwards in the cart.

The phantasmal man had evidently thrown some of his personal effects behind his seat—a club, a blanket, and the most beautiful thing Bronwyn had seen all day: a tall clay jug.

"Thank the gods!" she cried out as she held it aloft.

Snatching up the blanket, she carried the two items back to Gwynedd, tossing the blanket over her as she undid the cork and sniffed.

"What is it?" Gwynedd asked.

Bronwyn smiled. "Beer."

Royal Vagrancy

The forest gave way to a narrow valley a short while later. Gwynedd peeked out from under her blanket and peered over the driver's shoulder. In the distance, she could see a blurred smudge nestled in the foothills across the glen.

"It's a village," Bronwyn said. "About two miles distant. At this pace, we'll arrive in the late afternoon."

The cart jostled and shook as it rolled over the rough country highway. As they went, little paths joined the main road, and the ground became rutted with the deep grooves of wagon wheels. The wind flowed through the valley like a river current, carrying with it the smell of strange plants, pollen, and the musty scent of animal dung and dirt.

"Uh-oh," Bronwyn said. "I just thought of something."

Gwynedd retreated back under the blanket. "What?"

"The time of day. Gwynedd … I don't think we're on Iris."

Gwynedd scoffed, sticking a hand out from the blanket to grab the beer jug. She would have preferred wine, but the beer was better than nothing, and as far as ales went, it was rich and flavorful. "Not on Iris? Don't be silly. Where else would we be?"

Bronwyn pulled up the blanket and pointed to the horizon. "Look at the sky. We should be able to see the sisters at this time of day, but all I see is a sliver of gray. Gwynedd, how far could the Foxglove have taken us?"

"Maybe they're just behind us," Gwynedd said absently. "We can't see through the slope."

Bronwyn grumbled as she stood up. "I told you to get outside more," she said, shielding her eyes as she examined the sky. "The sun is past its zenith, and behind us. That means we're headed morning-way. The sisters should be on our left."

Gwynedd squinted at the sky, searching for the pale pink light of Iris's twin moons. Even through the daylight, her eyes told her they weren't to be found. "The power of the Foxglove is as close to infinite as magic can achieve," she said. "It might have taken us anywhere."

"It would explain our mystery driver," said Bronwyn. "And I think we can rule out an illusion. The more I think about it, I've never heard of a spell that drinks beer."

"But that wouldn't make any sense. The Foxglove's mission was to protect *our* world. Nothing would be served by taking us to another."

"You mean nothing that *we* considered," Bronwyn countered.

"And what do you mean by that?"

"Well, you told the council it would be a living weapon, right? Could it have decided to do this on its own?"

Gwynedd dismissed the thought and answered, "No. The Foxglove is alive, but not like you and me, or anyone else for that matter. It's a mixture ... a combination of the essence of the six races, and of every element in nature. Its power comes from a state of infinite connection. It doesn't have a mind like we do, nor any will of its own. I'm not even sure it would be aware of its intelligence."

"And if it were?"

"Then it would certainly be the smartest creature in existence, but with every mind in nature flowing through its head, it would probably go insane."

"Crazy enough to transport us to another world?"

Gwynedd scratched her head in frustration. "That's beside the point. You know as well as I do that magic cannot create life. The Foxglove is only a conduit. It focuses the life force of nature, but it's no more than a lens. It doesn't have thoughts."

"Oh," Bronwyn said, turning away to stare back out at the valley. "Never mind then, I guess."

Gwynedd eyed her friend suspiciously, studying her friend's sharp features: long green eyes set in skin tanned to the point of leather. They bloomed with subtle inner light, greener than the newest growth of the trees. A nervous tightness flitted about the edges of her expression.

Gwynedd could always tell when her day folk counterpart had something stuck in her craw. "What are you getting at?" she asked.

"I was just wondering if maybe the Foxglove didn't *want* to wipe out the Hava," Bronwyn said. "What if, in all that connection, with all that knowledge, it came up with its own plan? What if it sent us here on purpose?"

"To a different world?" Gwynedd said, cocking an eyebrow. "Where we can't help our people?"

"Well, what else is there?"

Gwynedd slumped into her seat. "I must have made a mistake. There's got to be some kind of error in the weapon's design."

"So sending us here was what? A misfire?"

"It's likely," Gwynedd muttered.

Guilt stung her heart. A hundred years in the making, the Foxglove represented the most ambitious project the Council Arcaneum ever attempted: the ultimate weapon to fight the Hava. It was her design, and apparently it had failed. All the suffering from this point forward fell squarely on her shoulders. Her conscience sagged beneath the knowledge.

The ground leveled out as they approached the borders of the town, and the cart gave a jolt as it lurched up onto the cobbled streets. Square and solid buildings framed their route, built on beams of heavy wood, hewn into shape and roughly planed. Their angled rooftops rose to steep peaks, where flower boxes and thick shutters decorated the windows.

"It's like a dwarf city," Gwynedd said, shielding her eyes to examine the blurred architecture. "But above the ground."

A loose crowd of workmen passed them by, chattering in a strange tongue.

"I don't understand the language," Bronwyn said.

"It doesn't matter," Gwynedd replied. "They can't hear us anyway, but obviously they're no illusion. Whatever's stopping us from communicating, it is something wrong with us."

The cart came to a halt outside a broad building, fronted by a pair of heavy wooden doors. A pair of tall windmills rose from the structure, pinwheeling the sky with sweeping arms of wood and canvas.

"A mill?" Bronwyn said.

The driver stood up on his seat and shouted at the mill's wide, wooden door. "Mach auf! Ich hab deine Lieferung!"

Gwynedd and Bronwyn exchanged a puzzled glance as the door slid open. A pair of workmen hauled the heavy wooden panels to the side. The driver cracked the reigns and the animals brayed, stamping as the cart rumbled forward. A dozen men began unloading the contents from the back as Gwynedd and Bronwyn leapt to the floor. Gwynedd tossed the blanket back into the cart, grateful to be out of the sun, and as her eyes adjusted, the interior of the cavernous space filled in.

Dust and motes of fibrous grist drifted through the air, flashing as they passed through scattered shafts of sunlight filtering in through tiny windows in the ceiling. Across a floor covered in straw, a pair of enormous grindstones turned in place, fixed to the cranks of the windmills overhead. A dozen men poured the grain into them through chutes mounted to a pair elevated balconies along the wall.

"Water," Bronwyn said, pointing. She reached up to set the jug of ale on the bench beside the driver.

They passed through the crowd like ghosts. The strange creatures took no notice of them as they made their way across the room to a table stacked with mugs beside a deep barrel.

"It doesn't look very clean," Gwynedd said, examining the water inside. She frowned as she watched one of the men on the balcony scratch his crotch before thrusting his hand back into a grain sack with a trowel. "It looks like they don't care much for sanitation."

"Beggars, aspire not to choice," said Bronwyn. She grabbed a mug and dipped it into the water, guzzling it down. She filled it again and drank it dry a second time before setting the mug aside.

"I suppose so," Gwynedd replied, following suit.

Two men approached as she went to fill her cup, but as she dipped it, the form of the vessel disbursed into the same fog that had afflicted Bronwyn's hand.

"I don't understand," Bronwyn said. "It worked a second ago."

The men filled their cups and left.

Bronwyn put her fingers in the water, and her fingers sent ripples across the surface. "Try again," she said.

Gwynedd did. This time, the water flowed into her cup without a problem.

Bronwyn huffed and leaned against the wall. "Now, that doesn't make any sense."

"No … " Gwynedd replied, holding the cup up in front of her face. "It makes perfect sense. Look." She pointed to the cart and driver. He appeared to be searching around his seat. "He can't see the jug."

Bronwyn stood up from the wall. "Hey, you're right!"

"There must be some sort of barrier between us," Gwynedd supposed. "A veil through which we can see and hear, but they cannot. When we touch something, it must come over to our side."

"And it can't go back?"

"Perhaps not. And it would seem that if we touch something where they are looking … we become immaterial."

Bronwyn retrieved her mug, face brightening as she held it up. "But that's good news!"

"How?" Gwynedd said.

"Well, it certainly *sounds* like magic, and if there's magic in this world, there's a chance we can use it to wake up the Foxglove."

Gwynedd cast her glance back to the Foxglove, still lying in the cart. "I hope so," she said. "If we really are on another world, it's our only way back."

Bronwyn strode over to the cart and dragged the construct out. Its feet gave a heavy thud against the floor. "Don't worry. You'll figure it out. You always do."

"I appreciate the vote of confidence," Gwynedd said as Bronwyn brought it over and went back for the ale jug. They sat down on a pile of grain sacks and stared across the room, passing the beer back and forth, watching the strange men go about their work.

Gwynedd began to laugh.

"What's funny?" Bronwyn said.

"Look at us," said Gwynedd. "Queens of the fair folk, and here we are, sitting on our butts in a glorified barn, drinking beer in the middle of the day like vagrants."

"Missing your palace?" Bronwyn said, taking a drink.

"Gods, yes," Gywnedd answered. "What I wouldn't give right now for a plate of mushrooms and a hot bath."

"And a fan," Bronwyn added. "And a fan-bearer."

They laughed, but their moment of reverie was cut short when a tall woman sprinted through the door, clad in sturdy leather and trailing a bright red cloak.

"Look!" Gwynedd said, dropping her cup.

The woman's eyes were long, and flashed green. Her skin was tan, and her hair fell behind her head to her waist in a long braid. The features were unmistakable.

"She's one of the day folk," Bronwyn said. "But here? With us?"

The cloaked woman dashed across the room.

"Hey! Wait!" Gwynedd called out, springing to her feet.

The woman turned, responding to the sound of her voice for half a heartbeat, before three more women came charging through the door behind her.

They were armed.

Woman in Red

The cloaked woman's pursuers were city folk as well, brandishing long knives, and one of them carried a bow. A long scar cut down the face of the first. She lunged to grab the cloaked woman, but with a deft roll, her target ducked and slid under a table, leaping to her feet on the other side, where she scrambled up a pile of crates. The second woman, this one wearing a black mask, gave chase, climbing the crates, struggling to follow the agile woman in red, while the first ran around to cut her off.

Jumping for the rafters, the cloaked woman hurled herself towards the ceiling, where she caught hold of the balcony overlooking the floor.

Bronwyn lifted an eyebrow. "She's certainly spry. Should we help her?"

Gwynedd drew her knife, a long triangular blade made from flint. "We don't know anything about her. What if they're the police? She could be a thief."

The red-cloaked woman ran along the second floor, but the scarred woman made it first to the bottom of the balcony stairs. She ran a thumb down the edge of her dagger and crept up the steps as the masked woman closed in from behind.

"Komm mit uns," the scarred woman said. "Das hier muss nicht bultig enden."

The red-clad woman yanked a short knife out of her belt. "Dafür wird Ranke dich umbringen."

The third woman, still on the ground floor, unslung her bow and readied an arrow.

"Whoever they are, they're speaking the same language as those strange people," Bronwyn said.

Gwynedd tensed. "They're going to kill her."

The red-cloaked woman backed away from her attackers, cornered on the balcony. For a moment, she glanced over the edge, contemplating a jump, but it was a long way to the ground.

The archer took aim.

Bronwyn hurled the jug of ale through the air. It broke against the archer's back, and she stumbled off balance. The arrow sailed wide across the room, striking the wall.

The scarred woman spun around and shouted, "Wer bist du?!"

"Let's just all calm down," Gwynedd said, putting out her arms.

Bronwyn drew her sword. "We don't want to hurt you."

The scarred woman spat and said, "Nimme beide mit."

They charged. The archer threw her bow aside and drew a dagger from her sleeve, diving towards Gwynedd. Gwynedd parried, pivoting on one foot to catch the woman's wrist. She brought her knife up and stabbed, aiming for the archer's gut, but the woman broke away before the blade struck. Twisting around, she brought her fist across Gwynedd's chin with a crack.

Stars flashed across Gwynedd's vision, and she staggered back, slashing her knife out in a wide circle. The archer snaked back in, stabbing towards her chest.

Bronwyn crashed into her, shoulder forward, and the archer went flying across the floor, dropping her knife as she rolled through the straw and dirt.

"Thanks," Gwynedd said, then her hand flew up. "Look out!"

The scarred woman came in from behind, drawing a long sword from a scabbard on her hip. The blade flashed down in a deadly arc as Bronwyn spun around, bringing her sword up to guard. Steel rang against steel as the two blades met. The scarred woman's sword slid down along Bronwyn's blade and turned, slicing her shoulder. Bronwyn hissed and jumped back, clutching her arm as Gwynedd lunged, ducking beneath Bronwyn's arms to deliver a vicious thrust to the woman's midsection. The stone blade buried itself in her ribs.

The scarred woman staggered back with a cough, dropping her sword as she clutched the blade. Bronwyn kicked her away, pulling her knife out as the woman fell backwards onto the floor.

Above, the masked woman closed in on the woman in red. The red-cloaked woman parried her first thrust and stabbed, but the masked woman sidestepped her attack and rushed in. Steel flashed through scattered sunlight. The woman in red jumped back, evading the strike, and brought her foot up in a swift kick, catching her enemy across the chin with a loud snap. She staggered back and the red-cloaked woman leapt on top of her. They grappled, wrestling in close quarters to the edge of the balcony until, with a shout, they fell over the side and tumbled over the side.

A steel edge glinted as the red-cloaked woman's knife came down. She stabbed once, twice, and finally left the knife in on the third stroke.

The archer stood up from the floor, flinching away.

"Ready to surrender?" Bronwyn said.

The woman dropped her weapon and ran, sprinting through the door and out of sight.

The red-cloaked woman wiped off her blade and put it away as Bronwyn and Gwynedd turned to face her. "Danke," she said.

Bronwyn gave a weak shrug and returned to the barrel by the wall. "Sorry," she said, taking up her cup to have a drink. "I don't understand a word you're saying."

The woman seemed to hesitate for a moment, keeping her eyes on the door as she approached, reaching out to take their hands.

Gwynedd exchanged a glance with Bronwyn. "What's she doing?"

"I don't know, but we might as well make nice."

The woman took each of their hands and shut her eyes. Gwynedd gasped as a strange sensation overtook her senses. Blackness and pressure surrounded her as the floor, walls, and the people of the building began to fade away.

"What's happening?" she shouted.

Bronwyn answered, "I don't know!"

Gwynedd tried to pull her hand away, but the woman's grip was like iron. With a desperate cry, she lashed out with her free hand, grabbing the Foxglove as the mill house and everything around them disappeared.

The Way Beneath

The village vanished, along with the crowded room and the bodies of the day folk on the floor. A lush forest stood in their place, even more vibrant than the glade they'd passed through to reach the strange race's city. Gwynedd looked around in wonder. Trees the size of the tallest towers of her homeland rose into the sky like dwarven megaliths, and flowers blanketed the ground in a dazzling carpet of saturated colors.

"Where are we?" Gwynedd whispered to the woman in red.

The woman squinted at her in puzzlement before putting her hand to her chest. "Rose," she said; then she pointed at Gywnedd.

"I think she wants to know your name," said Bronwyn.

Gwynedd put her hand to her chest and said, "Gwynedd."

"Gwyn-neth ... " the woman repeated, struggling with the pronunciation.

"And I'm Bronwyn," Bronwyn said, pointing to herself. "Bronwyn."

She flinched as her shoulder tightened.

Gwynedd examined her wound. "It's not bad," she said. "But we should find some way to clean it up and sew it shut."

"Sew it shut?!" Bronwyn replied, her jaw dropping.

"Best we can do without magic."

Rose pointed out into the woods. "Wir müssen los," she said. "Ich bringe euch in die Stadt. Ihr solltet mit Ranke reden."

"I'm sorry. I still don't understand, but my friend needs medicine," Gwynedd said. She pointed to the wound.

Rose leaned in close. "Das kriege ich hin, wenn wir es zu meiner Hütte schaffen," she said, poking at the cut.

Bronwyn winced. "Hey, stop that!"

Rose looked up at her with a playful smile. "Stell dich nicht so an." She reached into her pocket and drew out a roll of clean cloth, wrapping the wound tightly.

"Thanks," Bronwyn said, looking over Rose's work when she'd finished.

Rose gave her a clap on the other shoulder, turned, and began tramping through the brush.

Bronwyn looked over at Gwynedd and shrugged. "I guess we go."

Gwynedd dragged the Foxglove behind them as they made their way through the dense foliage. The forest reminded her of home. Deep greens and brilliant hues bloomed before her eyes as they hustled through the underbrush. Vines, dripping with sap and water, hung from the treetops, and a chorus of insects buzzed and rattled in her ears. Gwynedd's throat tightened with worry as she thought about the people of Iris. By now, the battle with the Hava would be over, and she dared not guess at her people's fate.

The trees parted to reveal a huge river spanned by a fallen log. Rose sprang across it like a mountain goat. Bronwyn picked up the Foxglove's feet with one hand, sharing the load as Gwynedd looked down into the frothing current. The spray from the rocks coated the mossy wood, and her boots threatened to slip with every step.

"We may have to learn this language," Bronwyn said, flinching as she stepped off the log and set down the Foxglove.

Gwynedd started dragging it again. "Hopefully we won't be here that long."

They emerged into a clearing a short while later, revealing a ramshackle cottage made from hunks of rock and mud woven with branches. Layers of sod and earth covered the roof, through which a tiny stone chimney emerged, sending a drift of fragrant smoke into the air.

"Bin wieder da!" the woman shouted.

A man in a tunic, red to match her cape, emerged from the door. He was tall and solidly built, a typical frame for a man of the day folk, with light brown hair falling down to his shoulders, bound in braided ribbons of red and yellow. He ran out to meet them through a thickly planted garden surrounding the hut. Rose took his arms as he approached, pulling him into a gentle kiss and a warm embrace.

"Du bist zu spät," he said.

The two of them shared a short conversation in their strange language before Rose stepped aside and the man put a hand on his chest.

"Amaranth," he said.

"Gwynedd," Gwynedd replied, pointing towards herself, and then at Bronwyn. "Bronwyn."

The two day folk led them inside, and Amaranth began hustling around the kitchen, assembling a pile of herbs and flowers on the counter.

Rose pulled a chair out from a wooden table, turned to Bronwyn, and said, "Setz dich."

Her meaning was evident enough. "Gladly," Bronwyn said, taking a seat.

Gwynedd rolled up Bronwyn's sleeve, revealing the bandage, already soaked with the green blood of the day folk.

Amaranth brought the pile of herbs over and began adding them to a mortar and pestle, along with a bowl of hot oil. The herbs popped and sizzled as he poured it over them, and the sharp smell of herbs and flowers quickly filled the room.

"What are they doing?" Bronwyn said.

"It must be some kind of medicine," Gwynedd replied.

The herbs and flowers dissolved as Rose sniffed over the mortar and gave a nod. Gwynedd was expecting her to rub it on the wound. Herbal medicine was archaic, but effective. At least it would fight infection.

Rose took up a knife from the table and cut the end of her thumb. She allowed a few drops to fall down into the bowl, and the mixture flashed. Gwynedd's eyes widened suddenly as, without a word, Rose picked up the mortar and poured the contents down her throat.

"What are you doing?!" Gwynedd said.

The woman seemed to shudder. As the next few seconds passed, darkness invaded her eyes and leached out to fill the veins of her face, as though her blood were infected with some kind of disease. A moment later, her palms bloomed with yellow-green light.

"Are you seeing what I'm seeing?" Bronwyn said.

"Magic," Gwynedd breathed, staring in wonder. "But how?"

Rose brought her palms down onto the wound. Bronwyn braced herself and clenched her teeth as the light in the woman's palms flashed.

"Does it hurt?" Gwynedd asked.

Bronwyn froze in her seat, watching the glow play in rivers across her shoulder. "No," she said. "I don't feel a thing."

There was a final pulse of light and Rose staggered back. Amaranth caught her, steadying her on her feet.

"The wound is gone," Bronwyn said, amazed.

Gwynedd gazed down at her healed skin and then glanced back at the Foxglove, leaning against the wall. "And we have a way home."

Queen of the Hill

Rose escorted them back into town, taking the lead, while Amaranth brought up the rear. Bronwyn couldn't help but remark inwardly that their march bore a striking to resemblance to prisoners being led about under armed guard. Gwynedd, beside her, walked in dreamlike silence. Bronwyn knew her well enough to suppose that she was still mulling over what they'd seen in the cottage.

Magic.

The trip back from the woods was as disorienting as the first. They still didn't know what kind of magic Rose was using—and there was no way for her to explain it—but it seemed to take them to and from another world. This time it took them back to the strange seventh race and their village in the valley.

"How long do you suppose this place has been here?" Bronwyn said, eying the cobbled streets and steeply pointed rooftops.

Gwynedd snapped out of her reverie and swept her eyes over the street. "I don't know. Some of these buildings look pretty old, but the architecture is primitive. This seventh race must not be very advanced."

A group of day folk passed them on the street, picking their way along the storefronts. Reaching in carefully, they plucked up fruits and vegetables and ate them as they walked. The same act repeated itself over and over as Rose and Amaranth took them up the road, leaving the strange race's shopkeepers baffled.

"They're all stealing," Bronwyn said, furrowing her brow as she witnessed the display. "What kind of society is this?"

Gwynedd watched as a young night folk girl snatched a biscuit from a tray.

"No society at all," said Gwynedd. "We've been here less than a day. Maybe the Foxglove brought these people with us. They're probably just as confused as we are."

Bronwyn looked up and her mouth fell open as they rounded a corner and emerged into a lamp lit square. "I don't think so," she said.

Ramshackle buildings piled up in front of them, stacked on the structures of the strange race's village. Bars, storehouses, and dormitories tucked themselves into the spaces between the hamlet's sharply-peaked roofs, rising layer after layer into the sky, linked by rickety catwalks, and joined to the ground by ladders and narrow wooden ramps. Day folk and night folk moved briskly up and down, descending from their rough-built homes to the streets of their unwitting hosts, foraging by plunder.

"I don't understand," Bronwyn said. "When did they build all this?"

The sun descended the horizon as they mounted a long ramp in the center of town, where a broad meeting hall squatted on top of the village's own town center.

"Do you suppose they've been copying them?" said Gwynedd.

Bronwyn pointed to a tall wooden post in the middle of the square. "Not quite."

Two day folk women hung from the post by their arms, knees bent with fatigue. Long slashes cut across their clothes, revealing grisly red stripes lashed deep into their skin.

A pair of guards met them at the meeting hall's heavy wooden door. Long tapestries hung on either side of the frame.

"Look at that," Gwynedd said. "These are the banners are from Iris. They hang them along the merchant's avenue."

Bronwyn put her hand out and held the fabric between her thumb and forefinger. The soft, familiar weave of silk slid through her touch like warm water. "I heard that the refugees collected them when we ordered the city evacuated, but we moved those people out of the capital weeks ago. What are they doing here?"

"None of this makes any sense," said Gwynedd, as Rose and Amaranth spoke with the guards. "Listen to them. That's not the language of the fair folk."

The doors opened, revealing three long tables in the center of a broad meeting room floor. A dozen day folk sat on benches beside them, feasting as they caroused to a raucous melody streaming down from a band stage on the left side of the room. Across from the door, a raised dais rose up, fronted by broad steps, and set with an ornate table piled high with roasted meat and vegetables. A muscled day folk woman stood behind it, easily six inches taller than Bronwyn herself, with more scars than smooth skin showing beneath her leather clothes.

Rose tugged gently at Bronwyn's sleeve and whispered in her ear. "Ranke."

The woman's boots thumped heavily against the wood as she came forward and Rose got down on one knee.

"I guess we know who's in charge," Bronwyn said.

Rose and Ranke shared a short conversation before Rose stood up and gestured for Bronwyn and Gwynedd to step forward. Ranke looked them up and down.

"It's a pleasure to meet you," Bronwyn said, bowing.

Ranke pointed to the floor in front of her. "Rose sagt, ihr habt sie gerettet, und dass ihr gute Kämpfer seid. Kniet nieder und schwört mit Treue, dann könnt ihr in meiner Stadt bleiben solange ihr wollt."

Bronwyn looked over at Gwynedd. "Did you get any of that?"

Gwynedd shook her head. "No."

Ranke waited, staring at them with her chin held high and her arms crossed. The men and women around the room got to their feet, faces grim in the torchlight as they watched. The last few wisps of sunlight drifted in through the windows, painting the ceiling with the final fires of the horizon.

Rose came over to them and spoke in a low voice. "Ihr müsst knien," she said, getting down on her knees. She bowed again in front of Ranke and gestured for the two of them to do the same.

Gwynedd turned to Bronwyn. "I've never sworn fealty to anyone in my life."

The crowd edged forward. Here and there, hands drifted to swords in scabbards, and lifted heavy clubs.

"I don't think there's much choice this time," Bronwyn said, getting to her knees and bowing low as she laid the

Foxglove down on the floor beside her. "Besides, if we can find a way to stick around here, you might be able to figure out how they work their magic. That has to be worth a few bended knees."

Gwynedd stiffened her brow as she knelt down and, after a reticent pause, bowed her head.

The crowd relaxed, and Ranke smiled, laughing as she pulled them back up to their feet and ushered them to the table on the dais. She carried on a one-way conversation for over an hour before the day folk began to weary and the party turned in for the night. Bronwyn followed Gwynedd outside to the railing as the sky began to fill with stars.

"Feel better now that the sun's gone down?" she asked.

Gwynedd leaned on the railing and sighed. "Much."

The city lights winked out one by one as the villagers went to bed. Over dinner, Ranke and Rose managed to explain in broken sentences and pantomime that the creatures of this world were called humans. Their city was Hane, and its settlements ran up and down the valley, following the river.

Bronwyn yawned and stretched. "I know you're better at night, but you've been awake for almost two days. You should get some sleep."

"You should too," Gwynedd said, keeping her eyes on the city. The night folk were moving about the town now, scavenging from the humans just as the day folk had done before sunset. "What do you suppose happened to them? To our people, I mean."

Bronwyn turned around and leaned on her elbows, propping her back against the rail. "I guess there's no way to know. Maybe the Foxglove did all this."

"Do you suppose it brought them all?"

"Maybe."

"And the dryads? The sprites? What of the other four races?"

Bronwyn straightened, put her hands on Gwynedd's shoulders, and turned her away from the city, staring into her eyes for a moment before pulling her close into a hug. "Don't worry, old friend," she whispered. "We'll figure it out. You don't have to understand it all now."

"But the people in the capital—"

"Will be fine. There's nothing we can do from here. We have to take our time, and figure out a way home. If we can't do that, we're no good to our friends anyway."

Rose emerged with Amaranth from the meeting hall. Gesturing for them to follow, Rose said, "Komme mit uns. Es gibt ein Haus in dem ihr bleiben könnt."

Bronwyn took Gwynedd's hand and led her along the catwalk after them. They followed the narrow wooden walkways until they came to a hut perched on top of a tinker's workshop.

"Not exactly the Council Arcaneum," Gwynedd said.

Bronwyn put her arm around Gwynedd's waist and gave her a little squeeze. "It's a start."

Rose stepped forward and pulled the door open. Simple furnishings adorned the dwelling's three rooms: a bedroom, a parlor, and a modest kitchen. A short staircase descended behind the back of the house, granting access to the tinker's basement. After a short farewell, Rose and Amaranth left them alone to rest.

"You can have the bed," Bronwyn said. "I'll take the couch. We'll see about finding another mattress in the morning."

Gwynedd went to the kitchen and tested the water pump. A slow trickle of water drained down into the sink. "It will be hard to work without the foundry's resources," she lamented.

"Don't worry," Bronwyn replied. "We'll have the place fixed up in no time. And besides, Rose healed my shoulder with nothing more than a few herbs and a stone bowl."

Gwynedd sat down and pulled off her shoes, slowly brightening up. "Maybe you're right. I built the Foxglove. It stands to reason that I can fix it, and at least we're not alone in the woods anymore."

"I like being alone in the woods," said Bronwyn, shedding her cloak. She unbuckled her sword and leaned it up against the wall.

Gwynedd laughed and got to her feet, heading for the back door.

"Not going to rest?" Bronwyn said.

"I'll never be able to fall asleep this late at night," Gwynedd said. "I'm going to check out the basement. Maybe I can convert it into a workshop."

Bronwyn flopped down on the couch and shut her eyes, throwing her cloak over her legs. "Suit yourself," she said. "I'll see you in the morning."

Gwynedd stopped in the door and said, "Bronwyn?"

She popped one eye open. "Yeah?"

"Thanks for cheering me up."

Bronwyn gave her a little wink and snuggled down into the couch cushions. "What are friends for?" she said, yawning. "And don't worry. I'm sure you'll have us out of here in no time."

Gwynedd headed downstairs. Between the two of them, Bronwyn could always be counted on for optimism, whether the situation warranted it or not.

The cellar doors groaned as Gwynedd threw them open. She could only hope that, this time, her friend was right.

A Year and a Day

Gwynedd sat up suddenly, startled awake by the metal clatter of pots and pans in the kitchen.

"Sorry!" Bronwyn called from the next room. "I was trying to be quiet, I swear."

Gwynedd squinted at the sun streaming in through the windows and rubbed her eyes. "It's all right. I needed to get up anyway." She looked down at her notes and the puddle of drool smeared across them. "Damn it," she mumbled, mopping it up with a handkerchief.

Bronwyn came through the door with a cast-iron pan in her hands. "Get up? What are you talking about? You were up all night. You have to sleep."

"I'll sleep when I'm dead."

Her friend set the pan down and came over to massage her shoulders. She looked over the notes and said, "Any luck?"

Gwynedd massaged her forehead and answered, "Not really, but I feel like I'm getting closer." She leafed through the myriad pages on her desk, stacked on top of each other in a disorganized heap. "It's just so frustrating. I've rediscovered hundreds of my old spells, but none of them seem to get a reaction out of the Foxglove."

Bronwyn took up the top page and read it. "The Earth Sight?"

"My latest attempt. Have you heard of it?"

"Only in passing. I had royal practitioner once who used to use it regularly." She handed the page back and looked out the window. "She died when we lost the western provinces. Gods … it feels like so long ago."

Gwynedd picked up a quill and scribbled down a few extra notes. "It's been over a year since we arrived," she said. "And I'm no closer."

Bronwyn took in a long breath and blew it out, shaking her head as she pulled her eyes away from the widow. "I'm sure you'll get it eventually," she said, forcing a smile. "If you leave your notes out, I'll copy them into my diary with the rest. Want something to eat? Tea?"

Gwynedd stretched in her chair. "What kind of tea?"

"Barley," Bronwyn answered. "I've already got the kettle on." Bronwyn said, setting a pan on the stove. She dropped in a few lumps of butter to fry up sliced zucchini and tomatoes, the latest batch from Rose and Amaranth's garden.

Gwynedd watched Bronwyn cook, listening to the fat sizzle in the pan. Her mother never taught her to cook, and when she took over the leadership of the night folk, the court and the counsel supplied her with everything she needed. There was something soothing about the sound that eased her exhaustion and settled her ragged nerves.

"Here," Bronwyn said, setting a plate of vegetables in front of her. "Eat."

Gwynedd did as she was told. Bronwyn sat down across the table, attacking her own plate like a hungry wolf.

"Are you in a hurry?" Gwynedd said.

Bronwyn shot her a sly grin. "Rose and I are heading to the cottage again. Amaranth says the crop is really coming in."

"Enough to satisfy Ranke?"

Bronwyn shoved a tomato into her mouth. "The baroness will get her tribute," she answered. "And there'll be more than enough left over for us."

Gwynedd speared a zucchini with her fork. She ate it with a smile and said, "That's good news."

"And not just for us," Bronwyn said, wiping her mouth on her sleeve. "Thanks to Rose, word about the Deep Veil is spreading. We don't have to leach off the humans anymore, and more and more people are foraging in the woods, or moving out of town completely to get out from under Ranke's thumb. If it weren't for the house and your workshop, we could get out of here too."

Gwynedd's smile disappeared mid-bite.

"Don't worry," said Bronwyn. "I didn't mean right now. You need the town, and we're doing fine. A little tribute is a small price to pay."

Gwynedd relaxed, finishing her breakfast with an uncomfortable helping of guilt. "I really appreciate the way you take care of me," she said. "I spend all my time working on this project, and I've got nothing to show for it."

Bronwyn reached across the table and took her hand. "The Foxglove is important. It's still our only way home. You just keep working, okay?"

Gwynedd squeezed her fingers and said, "Okay."

The kettle began to whistle. "Besides," Bronwyn added, getting up. "It's not as though I haven't enjoyed my time here."

Gwynedd gave a little chuckle as she moved from the kitchen to the couch. Gingerly, she extended a hand and flicked a set of undergarments—which she was fairly certain were Rose's—off the cushions. "Indeed," she said, taking a seat.

Bronwyn dashed in and scooped them off the floor. "Sorry. I meant to clean up."

"The three of you really should move in together," Gwynedd said, lifting a wry eyebrow.

"Ah, but then who would make you tea?" Bronwyn returned to the kitchen and cleared the table, returning with a pair of mugs. "We're just really good friends. That's all."

Gwynedd rolled her eyes. "Gods defend us from the appetites of the day folk."

"It's 'Faerie' here," said Bronwyn. "Or haven't you been practicing your German?"

"Yes, right," Gwynedd said, rolling her eyes. "And I'm an 'Erlkin.' You know, those words aren't even really German"

Bronwyn pulled on her boots and laced them up on a chair. "Give the locals some credit. They didn't even have language when they got here. We're lucky they came up with anything at all."

Gwynedd sipped her tea. Of course, her friend was right. It had taken some time—more time than Gwynedd would have liked to have spent—to learn the local language, but once they had, it was a simple task to learn the peculiar nature of the fair folk's arrival in the Veil.

The name held a double meaning. The Veil was the term the fair folk used for the invisible barrier that separated them from humanity, but it was also the term used to describe the strange world they inhabited, as well as its deeper layers. It descended away from ordinary reality, retreating from the mundane world like a road leading out to sea, until all that remained was the untamed wilderness to which increasing numbers had begun to migrate.

The Foxglove, it seemed, had dropped off the fair folk some fifty years before she and Bronwyn arrived. How it had managed the delay, Gwynedd had no idea, but the passage through the void had robbed the night and day folk of all their memories and skills, including language, and by all indications, the other four races had not been brought to the human world at all.

More than two decades of chaos followed the migration. The resulting civilization was barely a shadow of the society that, it seemed, now existed only in her own memory and that of her friend.

How far we have fallen, Gwynedd thought, finishing her tea. As to why the two of them retained their memories, there were no clues.

"You're sure you're not going to sleep?" Bronwyn asked.

"In a few hours, maybe," Gwynedd said. "I want to try a new preparation for the Earth Sight. Hopefully, this one will work, and if it does, I might finally be able to contact the Foxglove."

"You think it will?"

Gwynedd shrugged, gathering her things off the table. "Maybe. If there's a more powerful spell for connection in witchcraft, I've never heard of it."

Bronwyn paused, smiling coyly as she buttoned on her cloak.

"Arcanea," Gwynedd said rapidly. "I meant to say arcanea."

Witchcraft, another term borrowed from humanity: to describe the practice of magic. The fair folk term was arcanea.

"I told you it would happen eventually," Bronwyn said.

"I am not going native."

"It's inevitable."

"It is not."

"It's nothing to be ashamed of. We've been here a long time. We eat the food, live with the people, and speak the language. It's natural that some of their customs will bleed over into ours. Remember, we're the only ones who remember things any different."

"I still wish I knew why the Foxglove left us with our memories and no one else," Gwynedd said.

Bronwyn buckled on her sword. "Someone has to remember that there's a home to go back to."

There was a knock at the door, and Rose came through. "Good morning," she said, in German, and wrapped Bronwyn up in a tight hug.

"Morning, Rose," Gwynedd said dryly, switching to German to match.

Rose turned and put out a hand to give Gwynedd's shoulder a little shake. "Someone was up all night again."

"I'm always up all night," said Gwynedd.

"Well, up all day then."

Rose spun on her heels and turned to Bronwyn. "Amaranth is already at the cottage," she said. "He wanted to get a head start on the harvest."

"Trying to open up a little free time in the schedule?" said Bronwyn.

Rose gave her a little wink. "Maybe."

Gwynedd sank into the couch cushions with an agonized groan.

"Don't be jealous," Rose said, pulling Bronwyn into a kiss.

Looking at them, Gwynedd couldn't resist a little smile. Though she never passed on the opportunity to give the two women grief for their antics, it warmed her heart to see her friend as happy as she was.

"If you're stuck to each other, I can go down to the workshop and get a pry bar," she said.

Rose laughed. "You know, you could come with us. The garden is very peaceful, and it's not *all* fun and games."

Gwynedd drained her mug and stood up. "Thanks, but no thanks. I appreciate the invitation, but I've got too much work to do, and I wouldn't want to intrude. You kids go have fun." She leaned forward and gave Bronwyn a little kiss on the cheek. "And thanks for breakfast."

Bronwyn left with Rose. Stepping outside the door, they joined hands, shut their eyes, and vanished as they plunged down through the layers of the Veil, disappearing before her eyes like drifts of errant fog. Gwynedd gathered her notes and headed downstairs.

Partners in Crime

The back door of the house led to a tight staircase running down to a pair of cellar doors behind the tinker's shop. Gwynedd tucked her notes under one arm and the teapot in the other as she descended, gripping the handle of her empty mug with her little finger. The basement door groaned as she pulled it open and stepped carefully down a set of creaking stairs.

Beside a heavy stove, a table ran the length of the cramped space, stained with the juice and ichor of a thousand plants and animals. Mortars and pestles, burners, and half a dozen cast-iron pots covered its untidy surface. A stoutly built couch lay in the room's darkest corner, a reluctant concession to Bronwyn, who months ago had insisted that Gwynedd give herself someplace to collapse.

Gwynedd set her notes down on the table and lit a fire in the stove. A soft bloom of firelight trickled out into the room, warming the cool shadows of the cellar. Glistening bottles and jars filled a set of shelves along the wall, intermingled with the tinker's own supplies and equipment, some of which were presently disbursed into fine mist where the human and Veil objects overlapped. The tinker kept to the ground floor most of the time, but whenever he rooted through his stores, Gwynedd was inevitably forced to rearrange her own. Still, it was better than keeping her ingredients on the floor.

Returning to her notes, Gwynedd began compiling a list of materials for her latest attempt at the Earth Sight. The magic of this world didn't concern itself with willpower or focus; in the end, it was all about establishing a connection. The fair folk were not from Earth; they needed a link to the world before they could draw upon its power. As a result, the practice of magic had become a study in herb lore and chemistry, and spells, rather than efforts of intellect and concentration, could be consumed and used as easily as one could drink a glass of water.

The recipe was the hard part. Most preparations found their origins in the folk remedies and superstitions of the humans, but since their arrival magical practitioners among the fair folk had developed spells far beyond the medicines of humanity, who ironically weren't capable of any magic at all.

Regrettably, discovering the precise mixture of natural components required to forge the desired link was an agonizing process of trial and error, and most of the time, researching a new spell meant choking down several gallons of utterly ineffectual sludge.

Gwynedd bent down and fetched up a cutting board from under the table. With her list in one hand and a fresh cup of tea in the other, she retrieved her ingredients from the shelves and set to work.

Beef tallow, robin's eggs, salt, and a handful of rotten vegetables went into a pot, alongside a dozen ounces of gelatinous chicken stock. The mixture simmered and bubbled as it reduced, filling the room with a swamp fog of disgusting odors which Gwynedd barely noticed. After so many months, her nostrils had numbed to the stench.

Someone knocked on the cellar door.

"Come in!" Gwynedd called over her shoulder.

The door opened with a groan and a young Erlkin woman came down the staircase.

Night folk, Gwynedd thought, auditing her internal vocabulary. She disdained the humans' terminology, and made every effort to remind herself of the true names of things whenever possible.

Like most night folk women, she was tall and pale, sharply featured and thinly built. She unslung her backpack and slid it across the floor to the foot of the table, tossing her bleached leather jacket onto the floor.

"Hey, Gwinny," she said cheerfully.

Gwynedd regarded her with a raised eyebrow and a little smile. Her friend was barely nineteen, born in the Veil after the migration. "Hello, Lily," she said.

Gwynedd set down her knife and came around the table to the box. "Excellent. Were you able to find everything?"

"Everything," her friend replied, kneeling down to open up her pack. She tossed two lumpen bags of ingredients casually up onto the table. "I was traveling for six days to find the mushrooms you asked for."

"Why so far?" Gwynedd asked.

"There's a woman in Urach that sells foraged goods."

"Urach?"

"A human village three valleys over. It's also where I found these ... " She reached into her back pocket and produced a tall wooden case. "There's an apothecary on the high street who's going to be really missing this tomorrow."

Gwynedd reached into her robes and took out her money pouch. Currency had little value in a world where one could steal from humanity with ease, but Ranke controlled the fair folk's pilfering tightly, and poachers were severely punished. Gwynedd took out a handful of ration tickets and slid them across the table.

"Well, it's for the greater good," Gwynedd said, opening the case, revealing a length of coiled copper tubing. "I can use this to make a still."

"For what?"

"Isolating certain substances from body fluids and venom. Not all elements can be boiled to extract their essence."

Lilly took the money and stuffed it in her pocket. "Whatever you say," she said, perusing the ingredients on the table. "How's the project coming along, anyway?"

"Slowly," Gwynedd replied. "But hopefully this new equipment will help me find the answer."

Gwynedd began emptying Lily's bags: herbs, mushrooms, and several jars of insects—as well as their parts—found their way onto the table.

"You spend so much time working on that thing," said Lily, gesturing to the Foxglove, concealed under a blanket in the corner of the room. "You still haven't told me what it does."

"Only because I don't want to get your hopes up."

"Is it powerful magic?"

Gwynedd chuckled as she began to assemble the still. All the other pieces were already prepared. "Powerful enough to solve all our problems," she said. "That's what it was created to do, and one day soon, it will fulfill its promise."

"Sounds great," Lily said.

Gwynedd unsealed a jar and upended a pile of dead ants into the bulb at the base of the still. "Soon enough, we won't need ration tickets," she said, lighting the burner with a long match. "Or even weapons. That's the future I have in mind for you. For all of us."

Lily leaned down on the table, mystified by the liquid bubbling in the glass container. "I've been broke my whole life," she said. "I don't know what I'd do if I didn't have to spend all my time scraping by."

Gwynedd put a hand on her shoulder and squeezed gently. "Don't worry. You'll find something, and it will be what you were always meant to do."

"You must come from a pretty special place," Lily said.

Gwynedd glanced over at the Foxglove and answered, "Yes . . . very special."

Lily sprang up, wandering away from the table. "Do you mind if I crash on your couch?"

"Be my guest," Gwynedd replied.

Lily yawned and untied her hair, which fell in scraggly black waves to below her shoulders. "Thanks, and let me know if you need anything else from around the valleys. I feel like the sooner we get our hands on what you need, the better."

"Oh? Why is that?"

Lily lay down with a groan. "Word around village is that Ranke's getting restless. Too many people are leaving town, heading for the Deep Veil to start their own camps. If it keeps up, pretty soon there will be no one left for her to rule, and it's the same in the other towns. Some of the other baronesses have banned trading in goods from the Veil; in Jarlsburg, they outlawed Veil travel altogether."

Gwynedd started chopping up the next wave of ingredients. "History is filled with examples of leaders unwilling to give up their power," she said, slicing up a handful of Lily's mushrooms. They went into the pot. "The baronesses have been in charge for a long time. I don't know how they will maintain control if the people aren't dependent on them for food and the necessities of life."

"I don't know how they're going to stop it," Lily said, yawning as she kicked off her boots. "The word is out. The Deep Veil has something for everyone: food, shelter, better weather, and it's just too easy to get there."

"Just close your eyes and whistle, eh?" Gwynedd said.

"More or less. I've done it a few times. You kind of 'feel' your way there. It's hard to explain, but from what I've seen so far, I'm liable to move down myself."

"Instead of crashing on my couch?"

"I don't know about that," Lily replied, thumping the cushions with her palm. "It's a nice couch."

Gwynedd chuckled. "Well, maybe I can sell it to you."

Lily rolled over and tucked her face into the pillow. "Sold," she said, shutting her eyes. She mumbled, "Anyway, thanks for letting me stay."

Gwynedd regarded the sleeping woman with hidden pity and whispered, "Anytime."

There were countless men and women like her, living in poverty on the streets of Hane. Young fair folk, night folk and day folk alike, born into a life of rationing and servitude, laboring daily in the grip of leaders like Ranke. One day, she would take them all back to Iris, and the comforts of their true home.

In the meantime, Lily was right to be concerned. The days of poaching from humanity were drawing to a close, and with their passing, the power of the regional baronesses was dwindling away. It was not a transition likely to be peaceful, and the first entrepreneurs to plumb the riches of the Veil were set to bear the brunt of it.

The pot began to boil. Gwynedd lifted it off the stove and took it to the table, grimacing as she removed the lid. Drawing her stone knife out of her belt, she sliced her hand and allowed the cut to drain into the mixture. Blue night folk blood dripped down and the potion hissed, frothing as unearthly fire burned across its mottled surface. Gwynedd took up a ladle and dipped it into the cauldron. Holding her nose, she drank the potion and waited.

. . .

Nothing.

She dumped the pot out through a drain in the middle of the floor. No spell. Start again. She scribbled down her findings on a scrap of paper and began setting out a fresh batch of ingredients as Lily began to snore.

It was going to be a very long day.

Paradise Found

Bronwyn stuck her trowel into the ground and leaned up from the dirt. "That's sixty already," she said, glancing back at their wheelbarrow, full of potatoes. "And we haven't even gotten to the cucumbers."

"Or the carrots," Amaranth added.

Rose grinned, yanking a long, purple carrot out of the ground. She brushed it off on her shirt and chomped down on the end like a rabbit. "You know, I hear the Dutch are breeding these," she said.

"Breeding vegetables?" said Bronwyn. "What on earth for?"

"Different colors," Rose replied, taking another bite.

Bronwyn laughed. "Gods, I love the humans. They don't wash their hands but they've got time to redesign their vegetables."

Amaranth straightened up and cracked his back, looking over the rest of the patch. "I think we made our garden too big," he said, surveying the heaps of vegetables ripening on the vine. "We'll never go through all this."

Bronwyn picked up her trowel and dug down again, pulling up another potato. "We can take the rest back to town. Ranke will be thrilled. It's three times our quota. I don't even know how we're going to spend all the tickets."

Rose lay back on the dirt and smiled, wiping the sweat off her forehead with her sleeve. It left a muddy smudge. "Pretty soon, we won't even need ration tickets."

"Gods," Bronwyn said. "Wouldn't that be nice."

A moment passed in quiet as the three of them listened to the sound of the forest and the soft hum of the insects. A shower of warm rain began to fall, draining through the treetops like dew from the sun.

"Why do you always say that?" Rose said.

Bronwyn looked over at her, prostrate on the damp earth. "Say what?"

"Gods," Rose replied. "Like there's more than one."

Bronwyn pursed her lips, cursing inwardly. It was a foolish mistake. Most humans worshiped a single deity, and the fair folk of the Veil had no knowledge of their homeland's pantheon.

She and Gwynedd had chosen not to reveal their true origin, or their people's history. Assuming anyone believed them, there was no telling the kind of chaos and division such a revelation might inflict upon society. Wars had been fought over far less.

"It's just something I heard, before Gwynedd and I came to Germany," she said.

Rose sat up. "You must have seen some very strange things in your travels. I've never been more than a dozen miles from here. Amaranth and I came to Hane right after the migration, but of course we didn't know it at the time. We didn't know anything. Looking back, I can't even really remember what it felt like: no memory, no understanding. I don't even remember thinking like a person."

Amaranth picked up his hoe and began turning over the soil, tidying up the furrows. "I sometimes wonder if its how animals see the world. We weren't much different back then. Rose and I lived in a barn loft for . . . " he squinted, searching his memory. "Ten years? It's hard to say."

"It was a frightening time," Rose added. "We didn't even know how to speak until we learned the humans' language, and even after that, this whole region was controlled by gangs: bands of faeries during the day; patrols of Erlkin during the night. It wasn't safe to go out at all."

"It sounds like hell," Bronwyn replied. "Not like here."

"I guess it's a good thing you came to Hane when you did," said Rose.

Bronwyn sat back on her heels and inhaled deeply, taking in the smells of the garden and the forest. "It's true. If it weren't for your discovery, our people might have wandered the surface of the Veil forever, never knowing this other world existed."

Rose leaned up onto her elbows. "It wasn't my discovery."

"You were the first," said Amaranth.

"But I didn't discover the Deep Veil. It just came to me."

"You never did explain how it happened," Bronwyn said.

"There's not much to tell. I was sleeping in the woods one day, dreaming about . . . I don't remember, and when I woke up I was here. It took me hours to figure out how to get home. I didn't realize until later that it was my feelings that moved me."

"Still, quite a discovery," said Amaranth.

"A gift," Rose countered.

"Almost enough to make you believe in a higher power," Amaranth said. He shot Bronwyn a little wink. "Or several."

Bronwyn let her eyes drift up through the branches and gazed at the sunlit rain streaming through the leaves. The light reminded her of the liquid radiance she'd witnessed when Gwynedd first awakened the Foxglove a year ago in the chamber of the high seat. Her eyes watered and she said, "Or one."

"Do you really think this is paradise?" Rose asked.

Bronwyn pulled a ripe tomato off a nearby vine and bit into it. The juice sprayed out against her cheek. "No other name for it," she answered. "This forest can provide everything we need, and more. I only wish the humans had access to the same bounty. Their fields are barren compared to this."

"I'm not sure that's such a good idea," said Amaranth. "They breed like rabbits."

"Well, they have to," Rose said. "They only live fifty or sixty years, bless them. Can you imagine? It's already been fifty years since we arrived. We'd be nearly dead already."

"And you haven't aged a day," Amaranth joked.

Rose swatted him on the leg. "I wonder how old we really are," she mused.

Bronwyn pondered her question. The oldest person on Iris was a dryad called Teo, whose birth records indicated she was over three thousand years old. The oldest among the day folk—or faeries, to use the local term—lived to be at least half that age, but absent their memories, these people had no way of knowing how long their lives would carry on.

"It probably doesn't matter," Bronwyn finally said. "There's plenty to do around here to keep our minds off our mortality."

Rose gave a mischievous laugh and said, "Speaking of which, I think we've picked enough vegetables for today…"

She pulled Amaranth down onto the ground. He gave a muffled yelp as Bronwyn crawled over, fumbling with the ties on her shirt. She tossed it into the weeds.

The storm moved on a short while later, disbursing into scattered showers, and they sat naked on the front stoop of the cottage, relaxing as they sipped water out of wooden cups, filled from a rain barrel.

"I am covered in mud," Amaranth said.

"Well, it looks good on you," Rose replied with a giggle. She slapped a hand down on Bronwyn's muddied thigh. "And you've got a lot of energy. I don't know how you managed, especially after all that work in the garden."

Bronwyn lay against the door frame and returned a sated smile. "It's been a long time for me," she said.

"What are you talking about? We did this yesterday, and the day before that!"

"I meant before."

Rose snorted. "I find that hard to believe."

"It's true," Bronwyn said, sipping her water. "I lost my husband a long time ago. I haven't really felt for anyone since then."

Rose kissed her on the cheek. "That's sweet of you to say. I'm fond of you too." She paused for a moment before glancing over at Amaranth. She pinched him on the arm.

"Me too!" he said, blinking as he started awake. "Sorry, I'm just a little tired."

"We wear you out?" Bronwyn said, cocking a wry smile.

"You could say that."

Rose handed him her cup. "Could you get me some more water?"

"Me too," Bronwyn said.

"You two are so needy," Amaranth said, groaning as he got to his feet. His legs wobbled as he collected their cups and made his way to the rain barrel to fill them.

"You should feel lucky that such fine women have taken you into their confidence," Rose said.

"Just their confidence, eh?" he replied.

Rose gave a playful scoff, picked up a handful of dirt, and threw it at him.

"Hey!"

"That's for being fresh," she said.

He came back with their cups. Glancing up, he put a hand over his eyes and pointed into the distance. "There's another one," he said.

Bronwyn leaned forward to look. A long line of low shapes was moving through the brush. "Another caravan?"

"I'll get a blanket," said Rose, getting to her feet.

Amaranth waved her off. "It's alright. They're too far away to see us, but that's the third group this week. The Erlkin are all leaving the city for the Deep Veil. Rumor has it someone has found a layer where the sun never rises."

"Sounds perfect for them," Rose said.

He flopped back down into his seat. "I wonder what will happen when Ranke finds out."

"What can she do?" Rose said. "The old ways are dying. We don't have to live like beggars and thieves anymore, and I, for one, think that's a good thing."

A final roll of thunder emerged from the distance, and the caravan disappeared, descending deeper into the veil. Bronwyn frowned as she watched the figures vanish.

"What's wrong?" Rose asked.

She snapped out of her thoughts. "Nothing," she said.

Rose furrowed her brow. "Are you sure?"

Bronwyn paused, chewing the inside of her cheek as the last wisps of mist marking the Erlkin's passage disappeared. "Maybe," she said. "Ranke's a reasonable woman. It's just …"

"What?" said Rose.

"I've just never known a queen who was willing to give up her crown."

The Shape of Things to Come

A crowd filled the streets when they returned to town. Bronwyn and Rose wrestled with the wheelbarrow while Amaranth did his best to keep the vegetable sacks from tipping over the side.

"So many people," Rose said as they maneuvered through the throng.

Foreboding gossip filled the air, whispered between the townsfolk. Bronwyn strained her ears to listen. The baronesses had gathered, traveling from their home villages in the nearby valleys to meet with Ranke. Apparently, they were planning something big, and the fair folk of Hane packed themselves into the central square to hear the news.

The doors of the meeting hall groaned open and the guards ushered the three of them inside. Ranke sat on the dais in a silk robe, flanked by her concubines and surrounded by a dozen other women in formal attire. Amaranth steered the wheelbarrow around the side, where the quartermaster kept her office. Bronwyn craned her neck in a futile attempt to listen in as the woman slowly counted out their tribute and handed them their tickets.

"Hey! You can't take that!" Rose said.

Bronwyn's head snapped around. The guards were wheeling away the vegetables, including the portion beyond their quota.

Rose held the tickets up in front of the woman's face and gritted her teeth. "That food is ours," she said. "Our tribute is twenty pounds. Twenty. That wheelbarrow is three times that, at least!"

"Sorry," the woman said. "New rules. With all the goods coming in from the Deep Veil, we've had to adjust the tributes."

Rose's fist hit the table.

"It's alright," Amaranth said, jumping in.

Rose spun around and marched into the center of the room. "Ranke!" she shouted. "What's going on?!"

Ranke politely excused herself and stood up from the table, descending the dais. "It's good to see you, too," she said.

Rose squirmed out of her grip. "Ranke, they're taking all our food! We spent months growing those vegetables. You can't just change our tribute on a whim."

Ranke put a hand on her shoulder and offered a patronizing smile. "Now, you know that isn't true. This town is my home. All of you are my guests, but don't worry, I'm going to take care of you."

"So, we can keep our food?" Bronwyn asked.

Ranke clicked her tongue in her cheek. "I'm afraid not. Rules are rules. They're what keep our society in order. I can't be seen playing favorites with my subjects, but I can give you something else."

"Like what?" Rose said.

"How about one of my concubines?" Ranke offered, gesturing towards the men behind the table. "You have my personal guarantee that they will serve you well. Call it a gift, a thank-you for all your hard work."

"I already have a husband," said Rose.

Ranke gave a perfunctory nod. "Me too. He's ... " she scanned the faces of the men against the wall. "One of them," she finished with a shake of her head. "But it never hurts to have a spare. What do you say?"

"No thanks," Rose replied. "I need that food."

Ranke frowned. "I tell you what. We'll give you double rate for your produce this time, on account of the short notice."

Amaranth put a hand on Rose's elbow. "Let's just go," he whispered.

Rose shook him off. "It's not fair," she said. "Ranke, why are you doing this?"

The woman gave a broad shrug and put out her arms. "What choice do I have? With all these goods coming in from the Deep Veil, it's the only way to maintain law and order."

"Law and order?" said Bronwyn.

"Listen," Ranke replied, folding her hands behind her back. "We've built a community here, and it's my responsibility to protect it. We don't even know if this food is safe."

"Not safe?" Rose blurted out. "That's ridiculous!"

"And with people leaving the city in record numbers," Ranke continued, "we have to do everything we can to stick together." She pointed her thumb back towards the assembly at the table. "That's what the ladies and I are meeting about right now."

"But isn't that a good thing?" said Bronwyn. "People getting out on their own?"

Ranke sidled over and put an arm around her waist, steering her up onto the dais. "Bronwyn, you're an idealist. That's what I like about you, but the world out there is dangerous. We need to keep the people here, where it's safe, where we can make sure they're provided for. That's why, starting tomorrow night, travel through the layers of the Veil will be declared illegal. It's for the people's own safety."

"How can you stop them?" Bronwyn asked.

Ranke picked up a coil of thin, red rope from the table. "With this," she answered. "A gift from one of my new friends here."

Bronwyn glanced around the table at the faces of the other baronesses. They returned her glance with a dismissive stare.

"What is it?" Bronwyn said.

"It's rope," Ranke replied. "Treated with the juice of rowan berries. It stifles magic, and it stops people from traveling through the veil. It's the perfect solution, non-violent but effective. For now, we only have a few dozen yards, but eventually we'll have enough for the whole village."

"The whole village?"

"Wearing the thread will be mandatory, but don't worry, we're going to make it easy to adjust. I've already got people working on bracelets and necklaces. They're very stylish."

Bronwyn clenched her fist and murmured, "It's barbaric."

Ranke crossed her arms and drew in a tense breath. "Don't make this difficult, Bronwyn. This is going to happen. It has to, and it's only going to be harder if you make a scene." She reached into her pocket and took out a tiny, red bracelet. "Here," she said, holding it out. "Try it on."

Bronwyn's knuckles cracked.

Amaranth took a quiet step forward. "Bronwyn," he said, holding his breath. "Please … "

Bronwyn glanced back. Amaranth had his eyes on the exit. Rose's hand was already drifting towards the knife in her belt, but as Bronwyn looked around the room at the dozens of soldiers that surrounded them, she swallowed her rage and took the bracelet from Ranke's hand, slipping it onto her wrist.

"There," Ranke said, smiling. "That's not so bad."

They left the building with a few fistfuls of paper and an empty wheelbarrow.

"We'll have to get what we can from the cottage," Bronwyn muttered. "Before it's too late. We'll store the food in my basement until we find a better place. This is going to get worse before it gets better. We'll have to be prepared."

They carried on a few paces in silence, passing through the human crowd as they shut down their stalls and locked their doors for the night. The faeries moved among them to snatch a few final morsels.

Rose said, "The humans think the village is plagued by pilfering spirits. The region has become famous for it."

"We were destined for more than this," said Bronwyn. "The Deep Veil is our future. We can't let Ranke take it away."

Rose put a hand around her waist and stopped her, holding her close. "Don't worry," she said. "We will."

Rose and Amaranth went home. The kettle was boiling when Bronwyn made it back to her own place. Gwynedd was making tea.

"What happened?" she said as Bronwyn got out of her cloak. "I was expecting a huge pile of vegetables."

Bronwyn told her.

The kettle steamed as Gwynedd poured it over the tea in the pot. "I knew this would happen. Someone like Ranke isn't the type to let her power slip away. She'll destroy this society before she gives up control."

"We'll have to come up with something," Bronwyn said, pulling off her boots, exhausted. She lurched over to the couch and lay down. "Something wonderful is growing in the Deep Veil. Our people are building a new life. Ranke … she can't be allowed to stand in the way."

Gwynedd brought her a blanket. "Just don't get too attached," she said. "Remember, this is all just temporary."

"You're getting closer?"

Gwynedd tucked the blanket in around her friend and put a pillow behind her head. "Much closer," she said.

Bronwyn yawned and shut her eyes. Drowsy, she replied, "I wish there was a way to keep this. I don't want to give it up."

"I know," Gwynedd said.

"Do you ever wonder if this is what the Foxglove wanted for us all along? That maybe … " Another yawn. "Maybe we were never meant to go back?"

Gwynedd shook her head and answered, "I don't."

Bronwyn rolled over and buried her face in the couch cushions. "You should. Will you come with us to clean out the cottage tomorrow?"

Gwynedd laid a hand down lightly on her friend's shoulder and said, "I will. Now, go to sleep."

Bronwyn gave a muffled reply as Gwynedd stood up, collected the teapot, and returned to the basement.

The Space Between Things

Lily was standing over the cauldron when Gwynedd arrived. Crawling black slime filled the vessel to the brim, glistening with subtle waves of oily color just beneath the surface.

A bubble of noxious air rose to the surface of the cauldron and burst. Lily grimaced as she brought her thumb to her cheek to wipe away a fleck of the muck. The Foxglove leaned against the wall under a cloth.

"We'll have to do this alone," Gwynedd said, pulling the covering away. "Bronwyn won't be joining us."

Lily stopped stirring. "I thought you said you wanted her here as a witness."

Gwynedd put a hand on the Foxglove's cheek and murmured, "Bronwyn is too attached to this world. I don't think she wants to see how close we are to success. It's better for her if this happens while she's asleep."

"And what's going to happen, exactly?" said Lily.

"The Earth Sight will allow me to contact the Foxglove directly. Once I do, I can instruct it to fulfill its original purpose. We'll all be going ... " Gwynedd trailed off. Lily wasn't born on Iris, and revealing the full details of their home might be more than she could understand. "It will take us to a better place," Gwynedd finished, returning to the cauldron. "A safer place."

She stared down at the potion. Rainbow lights played beneath its surface, scattering and then gathering again to form strange, alien shapes.

"It doesn't look very appetizing," Lily said.

Gwynedd grabbed a ladle and dipped it in. "Hazards of the trade, but with a little luck, this will be the last time I have to do this."

Gwynedd poured the potion down her throat, tasting pond scum and rotten meat as the mixture curdled in her belly. A burning sensation invaded her eyes as the magic spread, beating against the insides of her skull like a mallet against an enormous drum. Gwynedd pitched back from the cauldron, clutching her temples as the strength in her legs gave way. She crumpled to the floor.

"Gwinny!" Lily shouted.

Gwynedd held out a hand and said, "I'm all right. Stay back!"

Black sludge bulged in her veins, and her eyes glossed over with black. Shuddering, she forced her arm to reach out to grab the edge of the table. Shaking, she pressed her eyes shut, only to have them snap open again with a gasp. Her gut churned, wriggling as the potion worked its way out into her body, carrying with it a dark energy that lashed across her skin like ice and lightning. Every muscle in her body spasmed as a tidal wave of sensation broke across her senses.

A moment later, everything was quiet. Gwynedd moved to stand, but instead, the floor fell away, and she found herself drifting, and it was as though the cellar had become a part of her own body. She could feel the stout legs of the table as though they were her own, and the cool weight of the ground pressing up beneath her feet. The popping of the fire in the stove crackled across her skin.

Lily knelt down beside her prostrate body, still lying in the middle of the floor. "Gwinny?" she whispered, gently shaking her. "Are you alright?"

The physical contact drew Gwynedd's mind briefly back into her own form, and she answered, "I'm here."

Lily picked her up. As she pulled her off the ground, the exertion of her muscles strained, echoing in Gwynedd's own arms.

"You're sure you're okay?" Lily said.

"Quite sure," Gwynedd replied, waving a hand in front of her face in a futile effort to scatter the impressions pouring into her mind. "It would seem that the potion was effective. This is the nature of the Earth Sight. It extends in all directions, passing through all minds, piercing distance and time to touch the substance of every part of nature."

The potion coated her like a spider web drenched in oil. "You look like a corpse," Lily said, cracking a smile.

Gwynedd leaned over the cauldron. Her reflection in its dusky surface revealed a face better suited to the grave than to a laboratory, and she staggered over to the Foxglove against the wall.

"So how does this work?" Lily asked.

"Your guess is as good as mine. When we built this weapon, all that was required was an effort of will, and the magic of its construction accomplished the rest. The magic of this world appears to require a more personal touch."

"It's a weapon?" Lily said.

Gwynedd laid her hand down on the smooth oak of the Foxglove's chest, brushing her fingertips against the rough patina of its hair, falling in green waves down over its shoulders. "Of a sort." She glanced back at her friend. "Whatever happens, do not try to stop what comes next."

Shutting her eyes, Gwynedd took a deep breath and relaxed her shoulders as she opened her mind. Her breath flowed in and out, cool and filled with the stone, musty smell of the cellar.

In and out. In and out.

Her fingertips trembled against the smooth warmth of the Foxglove's brow, detecting the subtle rivulets of metal and stone woven into its surface, following the patterns as they traced a path deeper into the construct's wooden form, entombed like glittering ore in rock.

And in those depths, her mind shuddered as the heart of the weapon pounded a single beat.

Power flooded into her thoughts as the heartbeat impacted deep in Gwynedd's chest, striking her with all the force of a falling star. Light burst across her vision, and her ears filled with a roar so loud that her head strained to hold itself intact.

When the lights dimmed, Gwynedd found herself in the Deep Veil, standing at the edge of a clearing in the woods. Flickering lights danced in the dark, and as the huge sound faded, terrified screams and cries of pain and anger rose up into the sky.

A scream pierced the blazing darkness, and up ahead, the telltale clang of steel against steel echoed through the trees. Gwynedd ran forward, bursting from the undergrowth . . . but the scene was peaceful. A cottage made from stone and mud, surrounded by a lush garden, squatted in the tall grass.

Rose's cottage, Gwynedd thought. *What am I doing here?*

Creeping to the window, she peered inside, glancing away as her eyes fell upon Bronwyn, Rose, and Amaranth intertwined. The Foxglove lay beside them, wrapped in a blanket on the floor.

Ignoring her friend's revels, she focused on the statue, and as she did, the wood of its body began to burn. The flames spread, consuming the furniture, the walls, and the floor. Lost in their passion, Bronwyn and the others appeared to be oblivious to the danger.

Gwynedd shouted a warning, but the three figures made no move to save themselves as the fire enveloped the structure. The window shattered, and Gwynedd jumped back as a wave of heat washed over her.

"Bronwyn!" she screamed. "Rose! Amaranth!"

The cottage was in flames. Gwynedd burst into tears as the roof of the structure caved in. A plume of fire and ash clawed its way into the sky, and from the blaze, a single figure stepped out onto the threshold, the dim silhouette of a woman clad in black.

"Ranke … " Gwynedd whispered.

The images vanished, and the basement snapped back into focus. Gwynedd collapsed onto the cold, stone floor.

"Gwinny!" Lily shouted, rushing to hold her. "Did it work? What happened?"

Gwynedd shook her head, stunned. "I don't know. I saw something, but … "

She trailed off.

"I'm sorry," Lily said.

Gwynedd rested her head on the young woman's shoulder. "Don't be. This is the closest I've ever come."

"Well, I think that's enough for one night. We'll try again tomorrow, okay?"

Holding up her shaking hands, Gwynedd glanced over at the Foxglove and breathed a sigh of relief. "Okay," she said. "Tomorrow."

They headed upstairs. Torches burned brightly along the empty streets as Ranke's soldiers moved through the town. The Erlkin in the streets gave them a wide berth as huge wagons full of lumber rolled out from the meeting hall.

"My friends say they're building guard towers," Lily said. "Hane is starting to look more like a prison than a town. You're sure your weapon can fix all this?"

Gwynedd held her hand. "I'm sure. I just need time."

The sound of hammers and cutting tools rose up into the night. Lily's hand tightened around Gwynedd's as she replied, "I just hope you've got enough."

The Greatest Good

Bronwyn burst out laughing. "It showed you what?"

Shrugging, Gwynedd looked away, suppressing a blush, and said, "I'm just telling you what I saw."

"Well, I hope we put on a good show," Rose said, cackling. She elbowed Amaranth in the ribs. "We've never been spied on before."

"I was not *spying*. It was a vision."

"I'll bet," said Rose.

Gwynedd rolled her eyes and grumbled, "I'm never going to live this down."

"Not a chance," Bronwyn said with a snort.

They were on their way back from the cottage, having cleaned out the garden in preparation for Ranke's new prohibitions. Gwynedd yawned and adjusted the heavy sack of carrots hanging over her shoulder. Under ordinary circumstances, she would have gone to bed hours ago, but something told her that the days where she and Bronwyn would be able to spend time together were rapidly coming to an end.

"Can we rest for a minute?" she said.

Bronwyn set down her wheelbarrow. "Yeah, we've got some time," she replied, cracking her back.

Their route had taken them to a hilltop outside the village, grassy, windswept, and strewn with boulders. The valley spread out before them, full of trees, homes, and farmland. Bronwyn stepped to the brow of the hill and took a long breath as Gwynedd drew up beside her.

"It's beautiful," Bronwyn said.

Gwynedd looked out across the landscape and answered, "I suppose."

Bronwyn cracked a smile. "Suppose?" she said, raising an eyebrow.

Gwynedd put a hand over her eyes and squinted. Giving up, she let her arms fall down and shut her watering eyes. "I miss Iris," she said.

Bronwyn gave her a little bump with her hips. "Me too, but this world isn't that bad, is it?"

"It's bad enough that we can't even take these groceries into town. We'll have to bury them in the woods, or find a cellar in a farmstead outside the city. I can't forgive the way things are, Bronwyn. Can't you remember what it was like? I can see the shadow of our home here, but it's like looking back on a dream, and every day that goes by, it gets a little harder to remember."

Rose strode up beside them. "What's harder to remember?"

Bronwyn glanced back and forth between them, stumbling as she searched for an answer.

"The place we come from," Gwynedd supplied. "Bronwyn and me."

"Ah."

"Can you honestly say you're happy with this place?" Gwynedd asked.

"It's a beginning," Bronwyn replied, surveying the valley like a general. "Not exactly a story book start, but nothing good ever came to anyone easily."

Gwynedd looked down at her hands and arms, still laced with the black sludge of the potion from the night before. "Well, you're right about that."

"Do you really think you saw the future?" Amaranth said, sitting down in the grass beside them.

Gwynedd set down her pack and took a seat on a nearby stone. "It's hard to say. The Earth Sight is rarely clear, and the visions it grants are often couched in symbolism and imagery drawn from the practitioner's own mind. I might have experienced something completely nonsensical, but something tells me there's a disaster on the horizon."

Rose took out her knife and fished an apple out of one of the bags. "I could have told you that," she said, slicing it. She popped a wedge of the fruit into her mouth. "Not exactly a stunning prophecy."

Gwynedd shot her a hard look, picked up her pack, and started walking. Bronwyn grabbed her wheelbarrow and set off after her.

"She didn't mean that quite the way it sounded," she said, keeping her voice low.

"She meant it," Gwynedd said.

"She just doesn't know you like I do."

"It's been a year."

"And you're always shut up in your lab. You haven't gotten to know these people. They don't see the value in the work you're doing."

"I don't want to get to know them," Gwynedd said. "I want to take them home, where they belong, and for all we know, when I do, they'll lose their memories again. There's no point."

"There *is* a point," said Bronwyn. "You can't go through life setting yourself apart."

"I can. There are more important things to focus on."

"Oh, yeah? What about Lily?"

"I don't sleep with Lily."

Bronwyn halted for a step and fell behind. Gwynedd kept walking. A few moments later, her friend jogged up again beside her.

"That was a cheap shot," she said.

Gwynedd felt a pang of guilt, but she stuffed it down as she recalled Bronwyn's words the previous night. "What about you?" she asked.

"Me?"

"Do you see value in the work I'm doing?"

Bronwyn chewed her cheek, all but confirming Gwynedd's suspicions. "I value that it's important to you," she finally said.

Gwynedd looked away from her. "I knew it."

"You've got to understand," Bronwyn said. "It's been a year, and the faeries are still my people. I respect that you believe your plan will work, but I also have to think about what they need now, just in case … "

She trailed off.

"In case what?" Gwynedd said.

Bronwyn cringed. "In case we never get home. In case the Foxglove did exactly what it was supposed to do, and saved our people, just . . . not in the way we expected." She ran around in front of Gwynedd. "I'm not saying you should give up. I want your plan to work, but I can't ignore what I feel, and my gut is telling me that coming to this world might not have been a mistake."

"And Ranke?" asked Gwynedd. "All the suffering? The thievery? Is that all part of our grand destiny too?"

Bronwyn took a breath. "It's a beginning. We can't only think about the past. We have to consider the future."

"A future without our culture, without our art, and without everything that made our people who they were," said Gwynedd. She stepped around Bronwyn and continued on in to the woods. "You want us to move back to the woods and live like animals," she continued, "and I want no part of it."

Bronwyn didn't follow her any further, and turned around to go and help Rose and Amaranth with the wheelbarrows.

Gwynedd watched her go, and her throat closed as a coil of regret and sadness tightened in her chest. Bronwyn didn't understand. Nothing had changed. The year was an illusion. Had she solved the problem within a week of their arrival, or a month, Bronwyn would have supported her without hesitation, but now ... her friend was fooled, taken in by superficial concerns and base temptation. Gwynedd cursed the Foxglove as she turned and walked on. Why could it not have simply done as it was meant to do?

The black smudge of the Earth Sight potion still tingled in her veins.

Very soon, it would. She would see to it.

Law and Order

Bronwyn slammed the door and yanked her rowan bracelet off her wrist, stomping around the living room as she headed for the kitchen.

"That's the third round of arrests this week," she said, opening a cupboard to retrieve a cup. She slammed it shut. "They've run out of grocers to spot check. They're all in jail. Now, they're rooting through the pantries of the cafes, checking for contraband. In another week, the meeting hall will be the only place to buy anything."

"I heard," Gwynedd said, keeping her eyes on her work, dissecting a rabbit Lily had pilfered from one of the human butchers. She'd have preferred a living specimen, but it seemed that, along with humans, higher-order mammals couldn't pass through the Veil barrier, and until they were dead, touching them caused a fair folk body to disperse in the same way they had already discovered.

Still, there was something about the creature's carcass that gave Gwynedd hope.

"What are you doing, anyway?" Bronwyn said, the tone of her voice still sharp.

Gwynedd drove a thin knife down into the rabbit's skull and split it open, revealing the brain. "I'm experimenting with adjustments to the Earth Sight. Hopefully, a better means of connection will reveal itself."

"Hopefully?"

Gwynedd gave an absent nod.

Bronwyn poured herself a cup of tea, the last of their supply. Gwynedd lamented the loss of the herbalist. She'd been arrested the previous week, and the last remnants of the vegetables and fruit they'd rescued from the garden had been used up for more than a month.

"You know, it's only a matter of time before they start searching our homes," Bronwyn said, opening a basket at the other end of the table to produce several hard lumps of bread. She dipped one into the tea and shoved it in her mouth. "If you think we've got problems now, wait and see what happens when they find your little workshop in the cellar. They'll drag you out into the square for the whips."

Gwynedd nodded again.

Bronwyn's fist hit the table, causing Gwynedd's knife to jump. It pierced the rabbit's brain and a drop of milky pink liquid spat up onto her cheek.

"Listen to me!" Bronwyn said.

Gwynedd took a long breath and leaned back in her chair, setting her knife aside. "I am listening. What's your point?"

"We have to do something!"

"What do you think this is?" Gwynedd shouted, gesturing to the bloody mess in front of her. "I'm working as fast as I can!"

Bronwyn began to pace, chewing her rock-hard biscuit.

Gwynedd could tell she had something specific on her mind. "You're planning to do something," she said. "Aren't you?"

Bronwyn abandoned her marathon across the floor and threw herself into a chair. "I'm going to meet with the rebels."

"Bronwyn, no."

"They've got weapons, and supplies, and the number of people who support them goes up every day this goes on."

"Ranke is too powerful."

"They're not going to fight her," said Bronwyn. "They going to start smuggling people out of the city. Once they're safely in the Deep Veil, there's no way to track them down. Ranke can have Hane. We don't need it anymore."

"Ranke's jails are full of people who've tried to sneak away," Gwynedd replied. "Most of them don't have the skills to survive in the Deep Veil. They end up getting caught trying to sneak back *into* the village. The Foxglove is a better solution."

Bronwyn clenched her fists, biting her tongue. Anger and frustration boiled behind her eyes.

"Go ahead," Gwynedd said. "Say it."

"The Foxglove isn't going to work. You asked me for time, and I gave it to you, but you're no closer to waking up that blasted statue. It's a hunk of wood. We might as well use it to prop open the door."

Gwynedd pushed the rabbit away across the table, leaving a trail of blood. "You don't believe in it."

Bronwyn leaned up against the wall and crossed her arms. "Not like you do."

"You did once."

"I still believe it brought us here for a reason," said Bronwyn. "This world is a gift, but it's up to us to fight for it. Gwynedd, Ranke isn't going to stop, and if we don't do something now, it will be too late. You can continue your research after this is over, when Ranke is gone, or when we're safe in the Deep Veil, or both! But I'm asking you, please, help me do this!"

The anger in her voice was gone. Gwynedd looked into Bronwyn's eyes and saw only desperation and sadness.

Gwynedd reflected on her friend's transformation with grim disappointment. Bronwyn's mind and heart were so clouded with the suffering of the present that she'd lost sight of the misery of the past: hundreds of thousands of their people, living for decades in fear on Iris, praying for salvation as the Hava closed in. On Earth, they had only traded their terror for ignorance, and Gwynedd found herself struggling to decide which was worse.

Someone screamed in the street, and Bronwyn went to the door. Gwynedd followed her, eyes tracing up and down her friend's back and shoulders. Her hair hung in tangles. No soap for washing. Her clothes were torn. No thread for mending. She was right about one thing, at least: the situation *was* deteriorating.

Ranke's thugs had three faeries on the ground, begging for mercy in the middle of the street, a husband and wife and their child. One of the soldiers waved a head of lettuce in front of the woman's face and threw it on the ground. Her boot came up and crashed down, grinding it into the cobbles. The people watched from the shadows of their drawn curtains, too terrified to intervene.

The railing of the catwalk cracked in Bronwyn's grip. "Are you coming with me or not?"

Gwynedd took a long breath. At the very least, she might be able to stop Bronwyn getting carried away. "I'll go," she said.

Bronwyn dropped down onto her elbows, leaning against the railing. She sighed with relief and said, "Thank you."

"Just to get a sense of them," Gwynedd added, "but you have to promise me that you won't get involved just because you're desperate to do something. We're the only people who remember the old world. We can't afford to die. Understand?"

Bronwyn took a breath and straightened up, massaging her neck with one hand. "All right," she said. "We'll be careful, but you have to promise me something too."

"And what's that?"

"That if it comes down to a choice between the Foxglove and our people, you'll remember that they are the reason we created it in the first place."

Dissident Voices

They met at Rose's cottage. A dozen or so Erlkin and faeries clustered in the cramped single room, hunched over a table. Bronwyn's eyes wandered to the corner, where a modest cache of supplies had been piled against the wall: jars of pickled vegetables and bags of dried fruit. Here and there, a blade hung from a belt, but most of them only carried knives and hatchets, the tools of frontier living.

"Gwinny?" a voice said behind them.

Gwynedd turned around. "Lily?"

Shew threw her arms around Gwynedd's shoulders and hugged her tight. "I didn't expect to see you here. I thought you'd be buried in your research."

"Bronwyn convinced me to take the night off."

"So are you going to help us?"

Gwynedd hesitated. "I haven't decided yet."

Rose entered the room, picking her way through the crowd to the table, where she unrolled a map inked onto a piece of cloth.

"I should have known this would be her idea," Gwynedd murmured.

Bronwyn shushed her as Rose explained her plan.

"She wants to use us as guides," Lily whispered, gesturing to the other Erlkin in the room. "We're out at night anyway, so we can collect the people who want to leave without raising suspicion."

Rose pointed to a spot on the map: the cottage.

"Once they're here, we'll sort them into groups and the guides will take them out to the base camps in the deeper layers," she said. "Everyone will be blindfolded while they're en route, so there's no chance of anyone retracing their steps and telling Ranke where we are."

"And we live at the base camps?" Bronwyn asked.

"Only temporarily," Rose answered. "Once the people are ready, we'll scatter them across the Deep Veil to build their own homesteads. The base camp will serve as a hub, where they can come to trade and look for help if they need instruction. Meanwhile, we bring down the next group. In a few months, there won't be a single faerie or Erlkin left in Hane, and without the citizens to support her, Ranke's hold on the city will crumble on its own."

Gwynedd leaned forward, studying Rose's drawing. "It won't work," she said.

Bronwyn lifted an eyebrow. "Why not?"

"It's too slow. You can't get everyone out of the city in one night, and doing something like this will only cause Ranke to tighten her grip. She'll turn the village into a fortress. No one will be able to leave again."

"So, what do you suggest we do?"

"Nothing," Gwynedd replied. "You need to stay hidden, bide your time, and wait for a better option to present itself."

Bronwyn threw up her hands. The Foxglove, again. Her friend was still wedded to the idea of stalling until she could wave her hand and solve everyone's problems. It was a fantasy that had already gone on far too long.

She put a hand on her friend's shoulder and said, "Can I speak with you for a moment in private?"

Rose exchanged a glance with her and leaned up from the table. "Everyone take a break. I'll be right back."

She followed them outside, where Bronwyn spun around on Gwynedd. "What the hell are you trying to do?" she asked.

"I'm being realistic," Gwynedd answered. "Ranke's position is too strong. She has the advantage of numbers, weaponry, and training. Fighting her will only make her stronger."

Bronwyn spat. "What a load of crap. You don't know any of that. You think you can predict the future?"

"Actually, I do," Gwynedd replied. "I saw the cottage burning in my vision, remember? There was a woman standing over the wreckage, dressed in black. It was Ranke."

"You don't know that for certain. The visions of the earth sight are cloudy. You said so yourself. They're obscured by subconscious thoughts and fears. We don't know what any of it means."

Gwynedd raised a quizzical eyebrow. "You think the image of the three of you dying in a burning building might be a metaphor for something good?"

Bronwyn blew out a humph and paced.

"The visions of the earth sight are indeed cloudy," Gwynedd said, "but they do not lie. If you carry on with this, something terrible is going to happen. I'm certain of it."

"But we can't just sit here! Ranke is getting stronger every day. Don't you see that time is running out? Soon, we'll be too weak to fight at all."

Gwynedd gave a slow shake of her head and said, "It is already too late to fight. It was too late from the moment we arrived. The Foxglove is our only hope now."

Bronwyn felt something snap. Her eyes widened and she shouted, "Will you shut up about the damn Foxglove!"

Someone poked their head out the door. "Everything alright?"

Rose waved them off. "It's fine. Go back inside."

"I'm sorry," Bronwyn said to Gwynedd, "but it's true. We're never going to get it to work. We need to stop investing in a path that has no future, and start fighting for what we have in the here and now."

"It's too great a risk. You're going to get caught."

"There'd be no risk at all if you came with us," Bronwyn replied. "With the Earth Sight, you can see the enemy coming from a mile away, and look into the minds of every person we recruit. Ranke's spies wouldn't have a chance. It would be easy!"

Gwynedd flung the idea aside. "It's not possible. I'm the only witch in Hane. Ranke would figure out what was happening and it would lead her to me. My work would be destroyed."

Bronwyn's chest heaved. She let out a frustrated grunt and kicked the nearest tree. "These people are ready to fight for their freedom, Gwynedd," she said. "Are you really telling me that you're going to sit in our basement while they're out there risking their lives?"

Gwynedd looked back at the cottage. "They're safe enough now," she said, "and they'll still be safe tomorrow. You're only going to make things worse by causing trouble."

"Well, at least I'm doing something productive."

Gwynedd looked at her with a cold glare. "Are you saying I'm not?"

Bronwyn choked back her retort.

"So that's how it is," Gwynedd said, straightening up. "You think what I'm doing is a waste of time. For the love of the gods, Bronwyn, do you think I don't know what you're going through? Do you think I don't care? Our people are suffering, but at least they aren't in danger. You used to believe that I could fix this. All you have to do is be patient."

"I've been patient!" Bronwyn shouted. "I was patient for a whole year! But even you have to admit that it's not working! This is the only option we have left!" She paused to take a long breath. "I'm sorry."

Gwynedd took a step back. "No … " she said.

Bronwyn reached out to take Gwynedd by the hand. "It's over."

"It is *not* over!" Gwynedd shot back, yanking her hand away. She spun around, shaking. "We do not belong here," she said. "This is not our home. This world is not our home!"

The cottage door creaked as Lily emerged. "Gwynedd?" she said quietly. "Is everything all right?"

Gwynedd strode up to her and took her hand. "I'm fine," she said. "Lily, come with me. I don't want you to have any part of this."

Lily looked back through the door at the crowd of people still gathered in the room. "But I want to help."

"Then help me," Gwynedd insisted. "You've seen my work. If I can finish it, none of this will be necessary."

Lily looked to Rose.

"It's your choice," Rose said.

A long moment passed before Lily let go of the door and crossed the garden to stand beside Gwynedd.

"You're being selfish," said Bronwyn.

"And you're being a fool," Gwynedd replied.

Bronwyn's thoughts swirled like boiling water, and she clenched and unclenched her firsts a dozen times as Gwynedd led Lily away.

"Bronwyn ... " Rose said. "I—"

"It's fine," Bronwyn cut her off, stomping back to the cottage. "Let's just get to work."

Silence

"I wonder how they're doing," Lily said.

Gwynedd sniffed over the bubbling mixture in the miniature cauldron. A dozen others lay scattered across the table and around the room, the unwashed results of countless failed experiments. "I'm sure they're fine," she said.

"Have you heard from any of them?"

Picking up a ladle, Gwynedd dipped it into the grey-green liquid and brought it to her lips. "Nothing, but if they were caught, I'm certain that we would be the first to know."

Lily watched her drink the potion and asked, "Why do you say that?"

The thick liquid burned as it slid down her throat, and Gwynedd gagged at the taste, a combination of vinegar, blood, and brine. "It's been three weeks, and nearly a hundred people have gone missing. If Bronwyn or Rose were caught, or seen, the first place Ranke would come looking is here."

Lily frowned and came back from the door to the table. "Not a very comforting thought."

Gwynedd felt a familiar itch as the magic stirred in her belly and spread into her limbs, coating her with a fine lace of blackened veins. Clouds of shadow fell across her vision as the already darkened basement descended into inky black.

"It wasn't meant to be," she said, as the impressions of the room drifted into her thoughts. "The people are deserting the true cause. The only cause. All we can do is hope that we finish this before our time runs out."

Gwynedd's perception drifted to the cluttered remnants of the potions scattered around the room. They were all variations on a theme, the Earth Sight potion, each with slightly different proportions of ingredients, prepared at different temperatures and stewed for different amounts of time. So far, none of them had brought her any closer to contacting the Foxglove.

Gwynedd sneered at it, propped up in the corner. It was meant to be the crowning achievement of a lifetime spent in the pursuit of a magic; instead, the construct was proving to be one of her greatest failures.

"Is it working?" Lily asked.

Approaching the Foxglove, Gwynedd answered, "We'll know soon enough."

She pulled the cloth away from its face and frowned, increasingly dissatisfied with the serenity of its features. Bronwyn believed it was some kind of supreme being, capable of its own thoughts and actions, but she was not a witch, and her understanding of the construct was limited. Such thoughts were better suited to the low creatures of the wilderness, lost and ignorant as they stared up at the stars and supposed them to be gods.

She laid her hands on the Foxglove's shoulders and leaned in to rest her forehead against its brow.

Awaken, she thought. *Your work is not yet finished.*

Gwynedd opened her mind, inviting the consciousness in. If she could but draw it out, she might seize upon its will, and if she could first gain a grip, the magic could do the rest. She would discover whatever strange defect lurked in her creation's expansive mind. There was no other option.

A long moment passed in silence.

"Nothing," she said, letting go of the statue. She stomped back to the table and slammed her hands down against it, but the gesture did little to quiet her frustration. She pounded the table again and again, until the objects on it rattled over and a jar flipped on its side, rolling off the edge to shatter on the floor. In a low voice, she said, "We'll have to try again."

Lily began to tidy up the pots.

"Don't bother with that," Gwynedd said, grabbing a fistful of herbs from a box. "There isn't time. Help me grind these up."

Old, Stupid Secrets

Bronwyn held up her hand, and the column halted, dropping to a crouch. Tense silence hung thick in the air, and she found her eyes darting rapidly from shadow to shadow, each time expecting to see one of Ranke's soldiers emerge from the brush.

Rose crept up beside her and whispered, "Everything alright?"

Bronwyn kept her eyes on the woods. "I'm not sure," she said. "I thought I heard something."

"The route should be clear," said Rose. "The guides checked it yesterday."

Nodding warily, Bronwyn scanned the trees and answered, "I know. Something just doesn't feel right."

A beetle the size of a small dog ambled across the path, emerging to cross the trail before burrowing back into the deep Veil's loamy soil. Bronwyn brought her hand down and the group resumed their advance.

"We're seeing those insects more and more," Rose said. "They're getting bigger. Ants, beetles, worms. No one has any idea how it's happening, but the foragers say they make for pretty good eating."

"Gwynedd would probably have a few ideas," Bronwyn said, recalling her friend's countless efforts to collect bizarre ingredients. It felt like ages since they'd last spoken, or even laid eyes on each other.

The refugees marched in silence.

"It's all right if you miss her," Rose said.

Bronwyn shot her a stiff glance. "I don't."

Her friend returned a coy smile and said, "Sure."

They marched through the brush. "Do you think she'll ever come around?" Rose said, cutting away a vine across the trail.

"Gwynedd? Not a chance. She'll never let the Foxglove out of her teeth," Bronwyn replied. "Even if she were the last person in Hane, even if we were to leave and come back in a hundred years, she would still be there in that damned basement, toiling away."

"You make it sound like she's gone mad."

Bronwyn swallowed a sigh and said, "Maybe she has. I just wish I'd caught it sooner. If I'd realized the effect her obsession was having on her, I might have been able to stop her before it was too late."

Someone cursed. Bronwyn glanced back to see a faerie woman picking herself up out of the dirt as the column moved on past them. She went back along the line and knelt down to help her gather her things. Rose followed her and kept watch, surveying the dense foliage.

"Maybe Amaranth can build her a hut," Rose said. "At least then she'd be close by."

Bronwyn gave her a little smile and kissed her on the cheek. "That's sweet of you, but Gywnedd is my problem, not yours. I'll get it all sorted out eventually. She just wants to focus, that's all. She hates distractions, and I think . . . " she paused, considering her words. "I think that deep down, she feels like all of this is her fault."

They finished gathering the woman's spilled belongings and hustled back up the trail.

"How could any of this be her fault?" Rose said.

Bronwyn turned away, dodging the question as they arrived at the front of the line.

"Bronwyn?" Rose said. "Is there something you're not telling me?"

Bronwyn stared ahead, trying to keep a straight face. It wasn't as though she didn't *want* to tell her, but they'd gone on for so long keeping their story a secret, it had become second nature not to explain. On the other hand, if she really had abandoned any hope of getting back to Iris, there was very little harm in it, and it didn't feel right to keep something so important from the woman who — at least now — was probably her closest friend.

"You two," Rose said, smiling. "You've always had something between you: your history, your friendship, and that ridiculous statue. It's like a mystery." She kissed Bronwyn on the cheek. "Maybe that's what caught my attention."

Truthfully, Bronwyn understood why Gwynedd fought so fiercely. Iris was still out there, and a civilization was a hard thing to leave behind. Gwynedd held onto it with the tenacity of a steel vise, as though if she loosened her grip even for an instant, the entire existence might slip away.

But as she stood beside her friend, escorting her people towards freedom and a new life, Bronwyn realized that perhaps, very soon, she at least would be ready to let it go.

"I'll tell you someday," Bronwyn said, putting a hand around her waist. "When all of this is over, and none of our old, stupid secrets matter anymore."

The path wound on into a dense thicket. Fallen leaves and pebbles covered the forest floor, and only a few faint wisps of moonlight penetrated the leaves overhead.

An infant began to cry behind them, hungry, and Bronwyn's ears picked up the whispered complaints of a young boy whose feet had begun to ache. There was no telling how much of the old culture would survive, carried over by her people's natural inclinations, but they would also never know the horror of the Hava, or the war that had ravaged their world. They would be happy here, and that had to count for something.

They turned a corner to find a pile of fallen logs blocking their path.

"I thought you said the guides checked this route?" Bronwyn said.

Rose pulled out her knife, dropping into a ready stance as her eyes darted to the trees. "They did."

Bronwyn ran to the logs and grunted, struggling to lift them out of the way, but the pile was eight feet high, and dozens of logs thick. The trunks bore the tell-tale signs of an axe's blow, with hewn chunks missing and clean cuts under the bark.

"They were chopped down," she said.

Rose's eyes went wide. "But that would mean..."

"Someone knows we're coming."

Bronwyn scrambled back down the logs as the underbrush began to rustle. Shadows broke from the trees, and Bronwyn threw Rose to the ground.

Fire and Screams

Bronwyn dove into cover as the whisper-crack of bowstrings snapped across the trail. Pain burst across her senses as she struck the ground, and her hand flew to her arm. Her hand closed around the shaft of an arrow embedded in her shoulder. Ranke's soldiers emerged from the trees, and the refugees panicked, fleeing back along the trail into the forest.

Bronwyn broke the shaft of the arrow off with a grunt as Rose crawled over.

"We have to get out of here!" Bronwyn shouted over the chaos. "Where is Amaranth?"

"At the back of the line! We have to find him!"

They looked up at the churning mass of fair folk, terrified as they scrambled, trampling each other to get away as the arrows rained down.

"Stay low," Bronwyn said, pulling herself up into a crouch. "We'll have to move fast."

Some of the refugees tried to climb over the logs in a bid to escape the confines of the ravine, only to be shot down as they neared the top. Bronwyn and Rose dashed along the edge of the crowd, ducking through the loose cover and boulders that lined the path. Ranke's people drew their blades as the caravan disbursed, moving in to cut off the refugees' retreat.

"How many of them are there?" Rose shouted.

"Too many!" Bronwyn called back as they ran.

She leapt over the fallen body of a young woman, only to trip on the body of another. Stumbling, she fell to the ground in the middle of a pile of bodies. Some of them were alive, bloodied and gasping as blood seeped from their wounds; most were dead, having already succumbed to the viciousness of the assault. Bronwyn clenched her teeth, forcing her anger down as she threw herself up from the ground and kept running.

Her face fell as the trees began to thin and they emerged from the thicket. A hundred shining blades flashed in the sparse moonlight, tightly gripped in black-gloved hands, and the forest filled in with long cloaks and hoods the color of crows.

Ranke was among them, hood pulled back as she laid waste to the fleeing throng. Dire ecstasy twisted her scarred features, and fresh blood ran down the length of her blade.

Bronwyn ducked behind a bush and pulled Rose in beside her. The refugees ran in every direction, frantic as they tried to escape. Most didn't make it past Ranke's soldiers; those few that did scattered, running blind as they disappeared into the trees, where the sounds of screams and agony echoed, withering in the dark.

"They're all around us," Bronwyn said.

Rose peered out from their hiding place. "I don't see Amaranth."

Bronwyn joined her in scanning the brush, when her eyes fell upon a tall man brawling with two soldiers wielding heavy, stone clubs. "There!" she said.

They broke from cover in a mad sprint to reach him. Bronwyn ran in behind one of the soldiers and jammed her sword into his back, impaling him through the heart. Rose jumped on the second, hanging around her neck to drag him to the ground. Her short knife glinted in the moonlight as she wrapped her legs around the woman's chest and brought it down in a deadly arc. The point buried itself in the soldier's throat and her last breath emerged through a gurgle of green blood.

The noise drew the attention of another group, and Amaranth readied his sword as they moved in. "Fight or run?" he said.

"You!" someone shouted. "Stop!"

An arrow streaked out the dark. Bronwyn pulled Rose up off the ground and answered, "Run."

They took off into the woods. "What the hell happened?" Amaranth called back over his shoulder.

"It's an ambush," Bronwyn replied, legs pumping. "They were waiting for us."

"But how?" said Rose. "No one knew the route except the guides."

"Maybe someone followed us," Amaranth said. "Did anybody see anything before we left town?"

Bronwyn glanced back over her shoulder at the carnage, cast in firelight, fading away behind them. "It doesn't matter," she said. "Let's just get out of here. We told the people to run and hide if anything went wrong. When this is over, we'll circle back and find as many as we can."

Her shoulder throbbed, and Bronwyn gripped the sound.

"We should head for the cottage," Rose said. "We'll be safe there until the dust settles."

Bronwyn shook her head as she jumped over a fallen log. "You two go. I have to get back to town."

Rose's head snapped around. "Back to town? They'll catch you!"

"I don't have a choice," Bronwyn said. "If they got this close, there's a chance that someone saw us. If they did, Ranke will go after Gwynedd to get to me. Someone has to warn her. I'll meet you later, okay?"

Rose and Amaranth exchanged glances. "Okay," they said.

They turned, sprinting off into the darkness. Bronwyn cleared her thoughts and thought of streets, fields, and human buildings. She felt herself rising up as a cloudy darkness overwhelmed her vision. She blinked, and when she opened her eyes, she found herself standing in an empty pasture outside Hane. Turning, she ran back towards the town.

There wasn't much time.

Saved

Gwynedd leaned over the stove, arms shaking with fatigue. Together, she and Lily watched the cauldron bubble.

"You should rest," Lily said.

Gwynedd scratched her cheek. The magic in her veins burned, and she grabbed a cloth to mop up the sweat from her brow. "No," she said. "I won't give up."

"Who's giving up? You can work later. Right now, you can barely stand."

Glancing at her notes, scattered across the table's surface, Gwynedd went to the shelves and grabbed a bottle of dried mushrooms. She threw one into a mortar and grabbed the stone pestle to grind it.

"And what's that for?" Lily said.

"The next batch," Gwynedd replied. "In case this one doesn't work."

Lily grabbed her shoulders and pulled her away. "Rest," she commanded. "You're no good to anyone if you pass out. When was the last time you ate? Or drank?"

Gwynedd shook her off. "I had some water before dinner."

"That was six hours ago."

Gwynedd finished with the mushroom and set the mortar aside. "I'm not stopping. You can sleep if you want."

Lily turned away, drifting to the Foxglove in the corner. She pulled the blanket aside and stared at it. "Will this thing really do what you say it will?" she said. "Will it fix everything?"

"It will," Gwynedd said, adding a carefully measured spoon of salt to a fresh cauldron. "No matter what Bronwyn says. The old world can still be saved. Everyone can be saved. It's worth paying any price."

Lily cocked her head to one side, still staring at the construct. "You keep saying this is going to take us to another place," she said. "But you talk about it like it's some kind of weapon. What is it?" She paused to glance back at Gwynedd. "I mean, what is it really?"

Gwynedd thought about telling her, but how do you tell someone that everything they've ever known is a farce, that their life is a poor facsimile of what it might have been, and that every place they've ever been is merely a crude copy of the world they were meant to know?

Would she even believe it? Gwynedd thought.

"It is a weapon," she ultimately said. "At least, that's what it was supposed to be. It was meant to destroy an ancient enemy of my people, but instead, it brought us to this place."

"And if you can fix it, you can stop Ranke?" Lily supposed.

Gwynedd gave her a weary smile and answered, "Something like that."

Lily started cleaning up the lab. "I hope Bronwyn is okay," she said, stacking up Gwynedd's notes.

Gwynedd lifted a jug of beef fat off the floor and started spooning the sludge into the cauldron. "She'll be fine."

The jug slipped out of her hands and crashed to the floor in a slurry of grimy fat and broken pottery. Gwynedd cursed. Grabbing a cloth and a bowl from the table, she knelt down to clean it up.

"Stop," Lily said. "I'll get it."

"No."

Lily knelt down in front of her. "You have to stop. You'll kill yourself like this."

Gwynedd's arms hung down at her sides, weakly gripping the cloth and bowl. She dropped the cloth, wobbling on her feet. Lily took the bowl and put it on the table before taking her to the couch in the corner.

"Just a few minutes," Gwynedd said, sitting down, resolve giving way to fatigue. "Then we get back to it."

"Fine," Lily said, pulling a blanket up to cover her. "A few minutes."

A heavy pounding thumped suddenly above their heads.

"Someone to see the tinker?" Lily said.

Gwynedd strained back to a sitting position. "Not this late. It has to be for us. Don't answer it."

Someone shouted, "Open up! We're here to search the house!"

Gwynedd put a finger to her lips.

The pounding got louder and the voice repeated, "Open up!"

Lily leaned in close. "They're going to break the door down."

"Let them," Gwynedd said. "There's nothing in the house. If we're lucky, they'll leave when they realize no one's home."

Gwynedd listened intently, eyes locked on the ceiling, listening for movement. "They're still above the tinker's shop," she whispered. "Hopefully they won't bother to come all the way down here."

The sound of breaking furniture crashed above their heads. Glass shattered against wood and plaster as the soldiers kicked open every door and tossed every cabinet in the place.

"I warned Bronwyn this would happen," Gwynedd murmured. "It was only a matter of time."

The noise upstairs began to fade, and Lily crept across the room to follow the sound. "They're leaving," she whispered.

Gwynedd stood up slowly, eyes probing the darkness as the footsteps passed through the house and descended the back stairs. She cursed, retreating into the shadows as Lily snuck up the stairs and locked the cellar door.

"Lily!" Gwynedd hissed as Lily slid back down and sank back into the corner. Gwynedd hustled over to her and pulled her knife out of her robes. Together, they crouched in the dark space beneath the steps.

The cellar doors shook.

"It's locked," someone said, the wood muffling their voice.

The door shook again. "Ranke said to check everywhere. Help me kick it in."

Lily pulled out a knife of her own as the wood began to crack. Heavy boots crunched against the lock until the planks splintered and broke, and four gloved hands yanked the door open.

Black cloth and hardened leather cloaked the forms of two soldiers as they came down the stairs. The steps creaked under their weight.

The first soldier gave a whistle of amazement and said, "Look at all this."

"It's some kind of workshop," the second replied. She went to the table and picked up a carving knife. "Ranke did say a witch lives here. One of the rebels."

Her partner crossed the room to the Foxglove. He pulled off the sheet and said, "What do you make of this?"

"It's just a piece of junk," the woman answered, picking her way through the clutter to join him. "Ranke will know what to do it." She slid a knife out from her belt and lifted it up, point aimed down at the Foxglove's forehead.

The blade came down.

"Don't touch that!" Gwynedd shouted, emerging from the corner. She held her knife out and the blade trembled, shaking in the fury of her grip.

The woman's dagger hovered over the Foxglove. "Cowering in the basement, eh?" she said, drawing the blade gently down the Foxglove's cheek. "Well, by the look of this place, you obviously have something to hide. Ranke told us to bring you in. Your friend's been caught smuggling people out of the city. She wants to know if you know anything about it."

"I don't," Gwynedd said.

The woman swept her hand around the room. "I find that hard to believe. This room is full of contraband."

Thugs, Gwynedd thought, throwing aside any lingering doubts she might have had about Bronwyn's embrace of this new so-called society. "Get out of here," she said, stepping aside to create a path to the door. "I'm busy."

The woman tightened her grip on her knife. "Not a chance. We're taking you into custody, and when we're

through with you, we'll come back to collect your stash."
She turned and faced the Foxglove. "Starting with this."

She brought her dagger up and stabbed it down into the Foxglove's neck.

"No!" Gwynedd shouted.

With a scream, Lily charged out of the shadows. The woman turned, but the point of her knife was stuck in the crook of the Foxglove's shoulder. Lily flung herself through the air and tackled her to the ground. The woman struggled, grabbing Lily's arms as her knife came down.

Gwynedd ran to help her, but the man jumped into her path. Drawing his sword, he brought it around in a wide arc, slashing. The blade struck the cauldron on the stove and the liquid hissed, splashing to the floor as Gwynedd rushed in, bringing her knife up. The stone point cut through his leathers and buried itself in his stomach. Green blood flowed out over the blade onto Gwynedd's shaking hands.

The woman brought an arm around, balling up her fist to deliver a heavy punch to Lily's face. Her jaw popped and she rolled off her onto the floor, gasping. Rolling to her feet, the woman kicked the knife out of her hand.

"Bitch!" she shouted, leaning down to stab her through the heart.

Gwynedd caught her arm from behind and yanked her back. They fell against the table with a thump, sending bottles and clay jars tumbling to the ground. Gwynedd brought up her knife, but the woman caught her wrist and twisted, smashing her hand against the table until she dropped it. She clamped her hands around Gwynedd's throat, and she thrashed, pinned to the table.

"Well," the woman said, pressing down. "I guess I don't have to bring you in after al—"

The blunt thump of a heavy blow cut short her words and she slumped, dropping to her knees as her eyes rolled back into her head. She collapsed onto the floor. Lily stood behind her, both hands gripping the heavy stone pestle from the mortar.

Gwynedd stood up, struggling to breath as she massaged her throat. "Thank you," she said, wheezing.

"What do we do with them?" Lily said. "If Ranke sent them, when they don't come back, she'll send someone to come and find them."

Gwynedd stared down at the bodies on the floor and the chaos strewn across the lab. Her face twisted, and her throat gagged shut to stuff down the swell of rage rising in her chest. Bronwyn ... She did this. Lily was right. All her work was about to be destroyed because her friend couldn't just leave well enough alone.

"Why didn't she just listen to me?" she snarled, rage rising in her voice as she screamed, "Why didn't she listen!"

Lily grabbed her arm and tugged. "Come on. We can gather up the rare ingredients and take them with us. If we go now, maybe we can make it to Bronwyn's cottage."

Gwynedd shook her off. "No!"

Lily grabbed her again. "We have to! Gwynedd, we can't stay here!"

She ran to the shelves and grabbed a bag, stuffing ingredients into the sack by the armload. Gwynedd shuffled over to the Foxglove and pulled the knife out of its neck, leaving behind a deep gouge at the base of the statue's collarbone and shoulder. The blade fell from her trembling fingers to the floor, where it landed beside the still-bleeding body of the male guard. His blood pooled, running across the floor to mingle with the spilled potion from the upset cauldron.

Gwynedd's eyes widened.

"Lily…" she said breathlessly.

The young woman turned. "What?"

"Stop."

She kept shoveling ingredients into the bag. "I can't stop. We have to leave."

Gwynedd lifted her eyes and smiled. "No, we don't."

Flesh and Blood

"It's so obvious. I must be an idiot not to have realized it before," Gwynedd said, lifting the man up onto the table. She swept the scattered ingredients off the surface to lay him out.

Lily put the bag down and picked her way across the cluttered floor. "Realized what?"

"The Earth Sight was never going to work, because its ingredients come from here. Beef tallow, egg shells, insects, mushrooms. A few drops of my blood, and they connect me to the world, but only to *this* world."

"This world?"

Gwynedd paused, thinking. She went to the stove and fed it. The red flames danced, reflecting in the dark pools of her eyes.

Perhaps there's no harm in telling her now.

"The Foxglove is not of this world," she said. "None of us are. The power of the Foxglove is the magic of our people. Only the same magic can take us back, but the

Earth Sight is not enough. No matter what we add to the spell, it will always be an ingredient from *this* world. The Foxglove needs something else." She said, picking up the carving knife from the table. "Something from home."

Blood spattered as she buried the blade in the man's chest, spilling across the table as Gwynedd sawed the blade back and forth. Lily covered her mouth and took a step back.

"That's disgusting," she said, gagging.

"You've seen me dismember a hundred animals on this table," Gwynedd said, reaching into the man's chest. She yanked out his heart and set it in a bowl.

Lily grimaced. "This is different."

Gwynedd cut down to the man's stomach and said, "It is not. Ranke's people are animals, living off the scraps of mankind. Meanwhile, Bronwyn wants to take our people back to the trees. None of them understand what I'm trying to do." She stabbed again, chopping through bone. A spurt of blood sprayed up onto her cheek. "I'm telling you, Lily, our people had *cities*. Our people had palaces whose towers reached the clouds, and roads that ran the length and breadth of a nation that spanned the globe from horizon to horizon. That is what I'm fighting for." She pulled the man's liver out onto the table. "And I'm willing to do whatever it takes."

Lily looked down at the bodies. "I don't think I can do this," she said, taking a step back.

I expected too much from her, Gwynedd thought. *I've expected too much from everyone.*

Her people were gone. All that remained were ignorants and fools, too degenerate to realize how small their existence has become. They didn't deserve the salvation she was offering, but they would have it, whether they wanted it or not.

She lifted a curved needle and stabbed it into the space behind the man's eye. "Fine," she said, extracting it. "Just watch the door."

A fresh cauldron soon bubbled, stewing on the heat, but this time, it wasn't full of herbs, mushrooms, and animal parts; it was seasoned with blood and entrails, and the brew flowed green in the pot. Gwynedd cut her hand and let her blood drop down into the liquid. The mixture frothed, blazing with emerald light, speckled with black, reducing down until it congealed into a thick sludge.

Lily eyed the mixture warily as a flash of green light danced across its surface. "Are you sure it's safe?" she asked.

Gwynedd picked up a ladle and filled it. "I don't know, but we are out of time," she answered, bringing it to her lips. "And the need is great."

A muddy chill slid down her throat as the liquid passed over her tongue, spreading as the magic filled her veins. It spread across her skin like a deluge of icy water, before sinking into her flesh. She shuddered as a fine black lace of magic filled her veins, blackened her eyes, and froze her beating heart to its very core.

No going back now, she thought.

The sound of breath rushed into Gwynedd's head as her thoughts unfurled, allowing the impressions of the world to flood her consciousness. Rising panic throughout the city raced along the streets; the guards, vicious and determined, tore open doors and turned the homes of the city into cluttered heaps while the families that dwelt within them huddled in fear. The wind of an approaching storm swept through the valley, and in the distance, the sound of thunder rolled over the mountains like a wave.

Power rippled across Gwynedd's body, filling her with terrible force, keening with inaudible sound and flashing with invisible light. It drove her to the ground. Her muscles twitched, and with every languid heartbeat, urgent pulses of strength and heat mingled with torrents of cold.

She stared at her hands and laughed, her pitch rising as her skin drained of color, waning to a pale, ivory white. The potion stained her veins, painting her with jagged rivulets of oily black, until her limbs more closely resembled marble than living flesh.

"Gwinny . . . " Lily said, taking a step back. "What's happening to you?"

Gwynedd rose to her feet as her voice emerged in a low rumble. "It's working," she said. "I can feel it."

Lily ran to the corner pulled the Foxglove out. Rocking it back and forth, she moved it to an open space in the center of the wall.

Gwynedd flowed across the room. The trailing edge of her robes followed her, gathering a cloud of shadow as she walked. Her every movement passed through the air like a drift of smoke, and the sound of every footstep echoed with the voice of a vast and nameless cave.

This time, she thought, staring at the Foxglove. *This time I will have you.*

Reaching out, she shut her eyes and put her hands on either side of the construct's face, gripping it firmly. For a moment, she felt nothing, but as the seconds passed, the surface of the Foxglove's face grew warm to the touch.

"It's working!" Lily said.

Gwynedd opened her eyes. White light shone through her fingers, creeping out from under her palms like light at the foot of a door. Smiling, she opened up her mind and emptied her thoughts, inviting the Foxglove in.

Fear gripped her, and sick revulsion forced its way down her throat as the first fluttering edges of the Foxglove's consciousness alighted on her senses. Gwynedd felt her grip on the construct waver for an instant as her own mind fought to push the feelings out.

Don't like what you see? Gwynedd thought, sneering at the construct. *Too bad.*

She tightened her hold, and the sphere of her perception swelled, reaching out in every direction: into the sky, down into the earth, and racing across the ground to the horizon and beyond. The reach of the Foxglove's mind saturated her thoughts, filling them with air, water, stone . . . the minds and bodies of every creature for a thousand miles. Strangely, the experience did not overwhelm her. Like a great bird, she glided through their collective consciousness. Their thoughts were a gentle chorus, and each of their souls, a flickering point of light.

And then the world retreated, fleeing into darkness as her thoughts collapsed on themselves, recoiling. Gwynedd fought to hold them, but the impressions of the world slipped through her fingers like bands of liquid silk.

"No!" she snarled.

A hand touched her shoulder and Lily's voice appeared in her ear. "What's wrong?"

The last wisps of the Foxglove's consciousness fled away, and the light vanished.

"What happened?" said Lily.

Gwynedd sank to the floor, staring down at her bloodied, blackened hands and clenched her fists. "It wasn't enough," she said, a dark shadow seizing on her malformed thoughts. *Any cost,* she thought, and said, "It needs more."

Lily ran to the table. "More what?"

Gwynedd looked up at her, darkness rising in the deep parts of her mind. She could just barely perceive the tiny flicker of light in the young woman's chest. Rising to her feet, she took a slow step towards her and answered, "Blood."

Primal Scream

Bronwyn crept along the streets, moving as quickly as she dared. Ranke's people were everywhere, turning the homes of the city inside out in a mad search for the so-called "rebels." It was a vicious ploy. In the end, all the search would accomplish was the confiscation of as much of the citizens' supplies as possible, and the arrest of anyone with the capacity for causing trouble.

Gwynedd was right. Their actions *had* triggered a crackdown. Perhaps they'd moved too quickly, or maybe something like this was always on its way, but they couldn't give up, and it was too late to turn back. All they could do now was run. They'd already smuggled hundreds of people out of the city, and there were more who had left before. It would take time to regroup, but eventually, they would come back for the rest.

The door to the house was open, slamming back and forth as the wind of the storm drove in. Bronwyn dashed across the street, leaping to grab the catwalk and pulled herself up, breath hissing through her teeth as her stricken shoulder tore and bled.

"Gywynedd?" She whispered as she entered the house. Their furniture lay in pieces on the floor; the cabinets and chests lay open, their contents scattered about the place in broken pieces. Bronwyn went to the bedroom and whispered again, "Gwynedd? Are you here?"

There was no answer.

Maybe she hid in the workshop, she thought, heading for the back of the house. The sound of a scream outside made her jump and she glanced out the window to see a group of guards was moving up the street. Sneaking to the back door, she opened it quietly and crept down the stairs, where she found the cellar door kicked in.

Throwing caution aside, she ran down the steps. "Gwynedd?" she called out. "Where are you?"

A voice answered from the shadows. "Here."

Bronwyn stepped forward into a haze of muddled light. Magic hung in the air like smoke, wafting in tendrils of green, blue, and black that clung to her skin. The cauldron on the stove hissed and slithered, absorbing any light that came near into a thick abyss of featureless black. Gwynedd stood over it.

"Gods … " Bronwyn whispered. "What happened to you?"

Gwynedd kept her eyes on the potion, watching the liquid shift and churn. Her eyes were solid black, sunk deep into her skull, and her skin stretched pale across her neck and shoulders like oil-soaked cloth, showing distended black veins and trembling muscles that shook like winter leaves. Blood soaked her clothing, covering her hands and arms in a grizzly pattern of viscera and gore.

"Don't worry," Gwynedd said, shuddering over the sickly brew. "I'm fine. In fact, I've never felt better."

"Did the guards come?" said Bronwyn. "Did they find you?"

"It doesn't matter," Gwynedd said.

"Doesn't matter?" said Bronwyn, throwing her arms out to display the room. "Look at this place! Look at yourself!"

"The blood isn't mine," Gwynedd replied.

Bronwyn took a step back and said, "Not yours?" She ran to the wall and lit one of the lamps. Dim, orange light flowed out across the room, revealing the dismembered bodies of two guards spread across the table.

Lily lay on the floor. Blue Erlkin blood stained her neck, congealed in a deep gash where her throat was cut.

Bronwyn's mouth fell slowly open. "Gwynedd ... what have you done?"

"It was the only way," Gwynedd answered darkly.

Her friend looked up from the potion with a ragged smile. "It's finished, Bronwyn," she said. "I've done it." Taking up a deep bowl, Gwynedd dipped it into the potion and held it out. The liquid shifted, moving on its own in the vessel. "This is our way home. We don't need to worry about Ranke, or the Hava, or anyone or anything else anymore."

She brought the bowl to her lips.

"Stop!" Bronwyn shouted, smacking it out of her hand. The bowl smashed on the floor. "Gwynedd, how could you do this? Lily loved you! She worshiped you!"

Gwynedd stared at the broken bowl on the ground, turning to Bronwyn with an animal snarl. "It was necessary! This is your fault! If you'd listened to me, none of this would have happened! I would have completed my work in peace! We could have bled volunteers, we could have bled Ranke's soldiers, we could have done anything we wanted!"

Pausing to take a breath, she finished. "Now, there is no time."

She grabbed another cup from the table and thrust it into the cauldron, yanking it to her lips and swallowing it before Bronwyn could react. Bronwyn looked on in horror as her features became even more withered as she consumed the dark mixture.

Gwynedd voice rolled around the room like thunder as she spoke. "Let it be finished."

She reached out to the Foxglove, and its body burst to life. Shimmering copper hair broke free from the green, rusted confines of the statue, and the wood blossomed with pure white light. The gems in its muscles glittered, and the threads of precious ore running through its form gleamed like fresh metal from the forge.

A shriek that shook the ground emerged from its open mouth as Gwynedd approached.

"Stop!" Bronwyn said. "Gwynedd, look at what you're doing! Look at its face. This isn't right!"

Her friend stormed across the floor towards the Foxglove, both hands grasping the air between them.

Bronwyn sprinted forward. "Stop!" she shouted, grabbing her from behind.

"Never!" Gwynedd hissed, thrashing. "This is all that matters!"

She ripped her knife out of her robes and twisted, bringing the vicious point of its long, triangular blade spearing down towards Bronwyn's neck. Bronwyn let go and jumped back, crashing into the stove as she drew her sword. The cauldron fell to the ground with a heavy, metallic gong.

"I don't want to hurt you," she said. "But I can't allow you to do this."

Gwynedd laughed, the tenor of her voice wavering in the mottled haze of light and dark. "You?" she said. "Are you going to stop me, Bronwyn? When we're this close?"

Bronwyn's fist trembled as she gripped her sword. "If I have to. You have to stop, Gwynedd, before it's too late."

She pointed past her to the shining construct. Its body shook, twisting in as it pressed its back against the wall, holding out its hands in a desperate attempt to keep Gwynedd at bay.

"Look," Bronwyn said. "It's terrified of you. There must be a reason. You told me it's not alive, that it has no mind, but *look* at it. There is something going on here that we don't understand. You have to wait until we have a chance to discover the truth, and this..." She pointed down at Lily's murdered body. "This cannot be the way!"

Gwynedd's face hardened as her mouth fell into a grim frown. "I'm done waiting," she said. "The time is now. I will not fail my people again."

She lifted an arm, and a tangle of thick roots burst from the ground, coiling around Bronwyn's legs as Gwynedd turned away. Bronwyn strained against them, hacking with her sword to break free. Gwynedd seized the Foxglove by the shoulders, and it cried out. The sound rattled the stones free from the walls.

Every guard in the city will be coming, Bronwyn thought with a curse. She brought her sword up and sent it slashing down, severing the roots. Sprinting across the room, she tackled Gwynedd to the floor.

"Get off me!" Gwynedd screamed, scrambling away. She drove an elbow into Bronwyn's wounded shoulder.

A shot of pain burst across Bronwyn's arm, and her grip came loose. Gwynedd broke free, and Bronwyn sprang into a crouch, only to be restrained as more roots cracked from the earth to cover her. The coiling plants tightened, ensnaring her hands and arms, tightening until they closed around Bronwyn's throat. Her sword fell out of her hand and clattered to the ground.

"Watch," Gwynedd said. "In the end, you will thank me for what I do here."

She took a step forward, dark resolution hardening across her grim features.

The cauldron came hurtling through the air, emerging from the field of light. It struck Gwynedd in the back of the head with a dull crack and carried on, smashing into the floor, where it rolled away with a low rumble.

Rose stood over her.

The roots withered, withdrawing into the earth as the magic in the room faded and the Foxglove fell to the floor, once again a statue of ordinary metal and wood.

"What are you doing here?" Bronwyn said. "I thought you were going to the cottage?"

Rose pulled her up and answered, "I decided you were too important to me to risk. I got worried. I'm sorry."

"Don't be sorry," Bronwyn said, picking up her sword. "I'm glad you got here when you did."

Rose pointed down at Gwynedd. "What do we do with her?"

Bronwyn knelt down and felt her friend's pulse. "She's all right."

"Do we bring her with us?"

Guilt tugged deep in Bronwyn's chest.

Standing up, she answered, "No. We have to take the Foxglove away from here, as far away as possible. With all the guards in the city, we'll be too slow if we try to carry them both."

"She'll be captured," Rose warned.

"We'll come back and rescue her," said Bronwyn. "Whatever it takes, but she and the Foxglove can never be allowed to come into contact again."

Rose went to the statue and picked it up. "You never did tell me what it does," she said.

Bronwyn helped her get it off the ground, grabbing the Foxglove by the feet. "Please … just help me get it out of here." she replied, suffering a final glance at Gwynedd's unconscious form. "When we get to the cottage, I'll explain everything."

Dark Accord

Gwynedd awoke to a kick in the ribs.
"Get up!" Ranke barked.
Gwynedd held up a hand, blinking her eyes against flickering torchlight. Ranke's people stood over her, weapons at the ready. Her eyes flicked to the corner, the table, and the wall. The lab was still in shambles, and the Foxglove was gone.
"Damn … " she groaned.
Ranke kicked her again and said, "On your feet."
Two of Ranke's soldiers leaned down and picked her up. She wobbled on her legs, weak from the magic, which had all but run its course. The last dregs of the potion still tingled in her veins, but the surge that had accompanied the spell had gone, and the echoes of its energy withered in her bones.
"Where is she?" Ranke said.

Gwynedd looked past Ranke to the floor. The cauldron had spilled. "I don't know," she said. "Rose was here. She knocked me out."

"You expect me to believe you didn't see her?"

"She came at me from behind."

Ranke slapped her across the face. "Not Rose! Bronwyn! Tell me where they've gone!"

"She didn't tell me where she went," Gwynedd said.

"You expect me to believe they attacked you? Do you take me for a fool?"

Gwynedd cracked a smile.

Ranke wandered to the half-empty shelves and ran a hand along their disheveled contents, tipping them onto the ground one by one. "I knew you would be trouble someday," she said. "I saw it in your eyes when you got on your knees in the middle of my floor. You looked at me like you were better than I am."

"I am better than you are," Gwynedd murmured.

One of the soldiers punched her in the gut and she doubled over, collapsing onto the floor. They picked her back up and held her by the shoulders.

"You really believe that, don't you?" Ranke said, returning to stand in front of her. She crossed her arms. "Why is that? What makes you so special compared to every other homeless Erlkin and Faerie that I've ever taken in?" She gestured to the broken shelves. "Maybe these? You think there aren't other witches in this valley? Other fighters? Other hunters and gatherers?"

"None like me," Gwynedd said.

Ranke snorted. "Whatever you say. I don't care anymore. I never should have trusted you. Now, you're causing problems for me, and that means you've got to go, along with your friend, and Rose, and Amaranth, and anyone else who thinks they can steal my followers away into the Veil."

Gwynedd's laughter echoed in the dank space, and the soldiers looked at her in wary shock, glancing at Ranke as her face slowly turned red.

"You think you can stop it?" said Gwyendd.

"It's easier than you think," Ranke replied, reaching behind her back. She unslung a spool of deep red rope and held it between her hands. "I know how to deal with trouble-makers. All you need are the right tools."

She tied the rowan thread around Gwynedd's wrists and cinched it tight.

Gwynedd's laughter subsided into a low chuckle. *What a farce,* she thought, straightening up.

"Your power is a joke," she said. "And so is your society. You live like rats, raiding the pantries of humanity while you build hovels on their rafters."

"Better than running away into the forest to sleep in a tent."

Gwynedd's eyes drifted to the empty space on the wall, formerly occupied by the Foxglove. Her notes and the diary were gone as well.

Bronwyn was wrong. There was only one way forward left, and she could not be allowed to destroy it.

"Perhaps," she said to Ranke, kneeling down to take up the cauldron. There were a few sips of the potion left inside, gathered in a pool at the bottom, far too little to control the Foxglove a second time.

But certainly enough to find it.

The soldiers tensed, raising their weapons. Ranke held up a hand and they stopped. "Put it down," she ordered.

Gwynedd held the cauldron in the crook of her arm. "Don't worry," she said. "I want to make a deal."

Ranke brought her hand down slowly. "A deal?"

"Bronwyn took something from me," Gwynedd said. "Something very important. Let me have it, and I will take you to them."

Ranke folded her arms in front of her. "I thought you said you didn't know where they were."

Gwynedd put her lips to the edge of the cauldron and tipped it back. The black liquid slid down the sides and crawled into her throat. "It's like you said," she replied, discarding the empty vessel. Her eyes blackened as her voice fell deep as her voice deepened. "All you need are the right tools."

A Love, Shared

"I don't believe it," said Amaranth.

Rose stared at the Foxglove, resting on the cottage floor. "All this time, and she's been trying to take us home."

Bronwyn rolled the statue up with a blanket. Rose had bandaged her arm, but the wound throbbed with her every move. "Unfortunately, the only way to reach it is to kill," she said, tying the bundle shut. "And there's something else. When Gywnedd tried to control it ... it was terrified."

"It sounds like Gwynedd was pretty terrifying at the time," Rose said.

Bronwyn sat back on her heels. "There's more to it than that. I saw its face, and it wasn't just a construct of magic. There was a mind behind its eyes. I've felt for a long time that the Foxglove might have had a plan when it brought the fair folk here. We may not know what it was, but we have to protect it."

"Then we have to take it away," Amaranth said. "Hide it somewhere, where she can't find it."

The door opened and one of the guides poked their head in. "Another group just arrived," she said. "That makes forty-one. We're still missing at least twenty."

Rose answered her with a frown. "It's been two hours. The others probably died during the attack, and we can't wait any longer. Split them up into groups and prepared to move out. We'll head for the base camps as soon as they're ready."

The door shut. "Twenty people," Amaranth said. "It's unforgivable. Men, women, children … "

A tear slid down his cheek.

"Ranke will get her reckoning," Rose said, holding him close. "But not tonight. For now, we have to make sure our people are safe."

She kissed his forehead and stood up, lifting him from the floor. Bronwyn watched them, memorizing that moment of tenderness, and her heart felt as thought it would tear in two. Theirs was a love she could share, but not long ago, she'd possessed a love of her own, not a passionate love, but an unerring companionship that had endured for hundreds of years, and . . . she'd neglected it. Now, her best friend was probably gone forever.

Suppressing tears, she came to the awful conclusion that, because of that mistake, she was going to lose Rose and Amaranth as well.

The cottage's shelves and cabinets lay bare, their contents raided to supply what would probably be the last group of refugees to leave Hane for a long time. Even the furniture was gone, knocked apart to become walking sticks, firewood, and frames for packs and litters. Only the gray stone walls remained, rough-hewn and stoic like the mouth of a shallow cave. A low fire burned in the barren hearth.

She reached into her pack, removing her diary. "This book contains all of Gwynedd's research, along with my personal account of our time here, and these ... " She drew out Gywnedd's notes. "These are her last spell: to control the Foxglove. I want you to take the diary with you. In time, its magic could be of great help."

"And those?" Amaranth said, pointing to the blood-stained pages.

Rose took Gwynedd's final notes and threw them in the fire. The paper burned to cinders and disappeared in the draft rushing up the flue. Bronwyn watched the ashes crumble and drift away.

"I've never seen such incredible magic," she said. "Gwynedd lost her mind in search of it."

Rose wrapped her arms around her. "It's all right. Something isn't worth keeping just because it's costly. At least this way, if she wants to try again, she'll have to start from scratch."

Bronwyn drew in a long breath and held Rose tightly. "You're right," she said, wiping a tear from her eye.

Amaranth opened the diary and looked inside. "What's this writing?" he said, flipping through the pages.

"The original language of the fair folk," Bronwyn replied.

"But how are we supposed to use it?" said Rose.

"Someday, I'll teach it to you," Bronwyn replied. "For now, you only need to keep it safe while I am gone."

"Gone?"

Bronwyn cast a foreboding glance towards the Foxglove, propped against the wall. "Gwynedd cannot be allowed to capture the Foxglove. I will take it far away and hide it."

Rose stuffed the diary into her pack. "We'll take it with us to the Deep Veil," she said. "She won't find us there."

Bronwyn shook her head. "It won't be enough. Gwynedd is dangerous, even without her research. Eventually, she will regain her magic, and use it to scour the length and breadth of Europe."

"Searching for the Foxglove," Amaranth said.

"But also for us, presuming that we know where it may be found. We cannot go with the other refugees. Doing so will only put them at risk."

"She's right," said Rose. "But I don't like the idea of running. Why don't we fight her? We could end it here and now."

"Gwynedd is too powerful," Bronwyn replied. "We got lucky before. The next time, she'll be prepared. Perhaps, in time, Gwynedd's ambition will cool, and she will give up this poisonous dream."

"That could be a long time," Rose said.

Bronwyn picked up the Foxglove and slung it over her back. "I have heard tell of a distant land, far to the west across the ocean the humans call the Atlantic. Go there, and hide. One day … " she hesitated, swallowing a sob before she finished. "One day, I will find you."

Rose set down her pack. "You're not coming?"

Bronwyn coughed. "I can't," she said, choking back tears. "The Foxglove's power is great. For Gwynedd, it will shine like a beacon across the globe. Our only chance is to stay one step ahead of her, and I won't put the two of you at risk."

"I don't mind the risk," said Rose. "You shouldn't have to face her alone."

Bronwyn felt a flush of warmth across her cheeks. "I appreciate that, but I'll be fine, and I've got an idea. Hopefully, I can take it someplace she won't be able to reach. Once I do, I'll follow you, but you can't wait. The sooner you leave, the better."

"But where will you take it?" Amaranth said.

"It's safer for you not to know, but if I am right, the being that dwells inside this statue is more than just alive. It is conscious, and has been planning for this moment from the beginning. With luck, the creature itself will be able to help me."

She turned to head out. "But you don't know," Rose said, catching her by the sleeve.

Bronwyn kissed her on the cheek and said, "Have faith. Everything's going to be alright."

Amaranth gathered up their things and slung his pack over his shoulder. "We should get going," he said.

Bronwyn stepped lightly across the floor and kissed him. His shoulders relaxed into her touch. "I wish the three of us had enjoyed more time together," she said, holding his hand.

He pulled her into a firm hug and said, "Me too."

A shout seized their attention. They ran to the door as firelight rose in the woods, and a dozen soldiers burst into the clearing.

Into the Woods

Bronwyn pointed to the back window. "Go, now," she said to Rose
"But the refugees!"
Bronwyn took up the Foxglove and opened the door. "Just go. I will see them safely away."
Amaranth ran to the window and threw up the sash, climbing through. He reached back to help Rose through the gap. She paused for a moment, framed against the woods, and looked back.
"Goodbye," she said, and disappeared.
Bronwyn drew her sword, tightened her grip on the Foxglove, and ran out.
Black cloth and blades surged into the clearing like the tide of a dark sea, flashing in moonlight. The refugees ran as the soldiers closed in, screaming as the guides scrambled to assemble their gear. They grabbed as many people as they could, vanishing in drifts of mist as they plunged into the Veil's deeper layers, but as many were left behind as

managed to escape. Terrified screams echoed in the flame-lit dark as the first blades began to fall.

Bronwyn raced forward, driving her shoulder into the back of a man bringing his sword up to slay a pair of Erlkin children, wailing in fear as they huddled in the arms of their mother. The soldier slid across the ground with a grunt. Standing over him, Bronwyn drove her sword into his chest, twisting the blade to drive the life from his lungs.

The Erlkin rushed to their feet and struggled to grab their belongings.

"Leave your things behind!" Bronwyn said, grabbing the woman by the shoulder. "Make for the deep Veil and hide! The guides will find you."

With a nod, the woman shut her eyes, holding her children by their hands tightly, and they vanished.

A pair of soldiers lunged out of the shadows, heavy clubs gripped tightly in their hands. Their heads dripped with fresh blue and green blood. Bronwyn dove as they brought their weapons down, iron heads striking the earth like boulders. Rolling, Bronwyn brought her sword up in a fierce thrust, piercing the first guard's armor through the leg to send her screaming to the earth. The second brought her club around for another swing. The weapon crunched against Bronwyn's bandaged shoulder. She cried out in pain as the joint cracked and the blow carried her backwards to the ground.

A voice rose up over the clamor. "Kill them all! Bring me their heads, and arms, and bloodied limbs. Leave none of them alive!"

Ranke strode into the clearing, twisted rage looming like towering flame behind her terrible advance. In her hands, she held a gleaming two-handed ax, and the crescent blade cut like the moon across the sky. She laughed, triumphant, as the refugees fled in panic into the night.

The soldier stepped in front of her, lifting her club up with both hands. "It's over for you," she said, and brought the weapon crashing down.

Bronwyn kicked out, and the woman's knees buckled with a sickening crack. Screaming in agony, she fell to the earth, dropping her weapon as she clutched her at her shattered limbs. Bronwyn jumped to her feet and made a break for the edge of the clearing, weaving through the churning mass of steel and death, praying that the confusion and the chaos would offer her a few, fleeting moments to escape.

The cottage exploded. Rock and stone hurtled through the air, spraying out across the clearing in an avalanche of boulders, burning wood, and smoke. The force drove Bronwyn to the ground, and she scrambled to regain her footing as she cast a final, fateful glance back into the fray.

Gwynedd stood alone in the chaos, emerging from the fire of the cottage like a creature of pure darkness. Hot wind blew in great gales through the forest, while overhead, storm clouds covered over the sky, and flashes of lightning blotted out the stars. Bronwyn's heart trembled and her breath stuck in her throat as her friend marched through the flames, her dark blue robes soaked black with blood and soot.

"A woman in black," Bronwyn whispered. "It was you. Gods, my friend. I am so sorry."

Gwynedd's voice pierced the flaming dark. "Find her! Bring me the statue!"

The guards fanned out, scything through the crowd. Blood of Erlkin and Faeries flowed over the ground, a flood of terror, pain, and death.

Bronwyn picked up the Foxglove and ran.

Into the Wind

Bronwyn held her shoulder, wincing as she made her way up the long, shallow slope to the hilltop overlooking Hane. The storm boiled overhead, spending its fury in flashes of lighting, thunder, and a driving wind that threatened to bring down the trees. Glancing back, the sounds of the battle had faded, left behind when she moved from the deeper layers of the Veil to the surface.

Gods, I hope this works, she thought.

She focused her thoughts on the humans, on their city, their world, and their way of thinking, pressing herself as tightly as she could against the barrier that separated humanity from the fair folk, and praying that the Foxglove possessed the consciousness to understand her intent.

The trees parted as the cliff came into view. Ahead, the valley lay out across the landscape, dotted with the twinkling lights of Hane and the farms that circled its environs. They would never know the tragedy that had unfolded before their eyes, an invisible stage show of tyranny, betrayal, and death.

Bronwyn unslung the Foxglove and laid it on the ground.

"All right," she said, laying a hand on its shoulder. "I need you to help me. I can't do this without you, so ... wake up."

The statue was unmoved.

Damn it, Bronwyn cursed, shutting her eyes.

It knew, she supposed. It must have known, all along, that this would be its fate. From the moment it refused to destroy the Hava and spirited the fair folk away to this world, its infinite knowledge and limitless vision cannot have failed to anticipate this course.

Time is running out, she thought. *You have to go. Our people aren't ready for what you represent.*

Again, nothing.

Bronwyn took a long breath, struggling to reach out to the Foxglove's dormant consciousness, opening her mind to ... she didn't know. In the back of her thoughts, she cursed the many days she'd spent skipping school to go ranging in the woods, playing at slaying dragons while better students like Gwynedd remained in the library to study and learn the ways of magic.

The world needs warriors too, she thought, re-examining her oft-repeated phrase before murmuring aloud, "But not today."

She glanced back down the hill. A flicker of torchlight answered her gaze, still couched in the trees. Gwynedd would be coming. Her magic had led Ranke to the cottage; it would certainly bring her here.

Gwynedd's magic, she thought. *Of course.*

Gritting her teeth, she pressed her hand deep into her bandaged arm. Her palm emerged green, and she placed it on the Foxglove's shoulder, holding it as though greeting an old friend.

"Please," she said aloud, shutting her eyes again. She relaxed her straining mind. "There's no time left."

The Foxglove stirred, trembling beneath her fingertips as Bronwyn felt a calming warmth bloom beneath her palm. Opening her eyes, she beheld the construct's face, flickering with light as rivulets of magic coursed along the veins of gemstone that lined its graven surface. When its eyes opened, they pierced the night with pure white fire.

"Thank the gods," Bronwyn said, staring in awe as the creature rose to float above the ground, borne aloft by an unseen force.

It put out a hand, palm upwards, to Bronwyn, who put out a hand in return.

"What do I do?" she said.

Before her eyes, the body of the Foxglove began to change, wreathed in light as it brought its knees up and its arms around to hold them like a child unborn. A flash of light blinded her, and she turned away, shielding her eyes as the construct disappeared. A moment later, the fluttering seed of a maple tree alighted on her outstretched palm.

Bronwyn took it delicately, holding it out as she stepped to the edge of the cliff, and it was as though the air bent around her fingers, and a strange, rainbow light gathered on her arm, until finally, with a broken chord of twinkling music, the light dispersed. Bronwyn felt her hand pass through a slender gap, piercing a curtain too fine to catch the eye.

In that instant, Bronwyn saw a face. It flashed across her thoughts, alighting for a moment on her consciousness amid a swirl of strange images: a woman, lost in the woods; a city cradled in the arms of a great tree, and a civilization across the sea, reaching for the clouds on towers of steel and glass.

She let go of the seed, and the wind snatched it up, carrying it away into the storm.

And Farewell to Old Friends

Gwynedd emerged from the trees. Climbing to the hilltop, she stood behind her friend. The Foxglove was nowhere in sight.

"It's no use," Bronwyn said, staring out from the cliff. "It's gone."

Gwynedd's eyes flew open wide and she ran to the edge of the ridge, staring down the rocky, wooded decline. Her eyes saw nothing, and the pull of her magic only directed her only out into the air.

"What have you done?" she shouted.

"I sent the Foxglove to the human world," said Bronwyn, wobbling on her feet. "This is our home now."

"No!" Gywnedd screamed, desperation tearing at her throat. "It will never be their home! Their home is Iris! Our home is Iris!"

Bronwyn put a hand on her shoulder gently. "Not any longer. Iris belongs to the Hava. That fate was sure enough before you even conceived of the Foxglove."

Gwynedd smacked her hand away and said, "The Foxglove was a failure!"

"No," Bronwyn insisted. "You built the Foxglove to save our people, and it *did* save them."

Gwynedd clenched her teeth, rejecting her friend's words the moment they left her mouth. "I built the Foxglove to destroy the Hava, to save our *world*. Our people are more than flesh and blood, Bronwyn. Where do you see their culture here? Where is our art? Our music? Where is our history?"

"They will come. We will build a new history, unstained by centuries of conflict with a horror that these people will never know."

Gwynedd paced, her mind racing. Perhaps the Foxglove wasn't far away. Bronwyn might have thrown it over the cliff, or hidden it down below. Perhaps it could still be found.

Or her friends, she thought.

"How?" she said. "How did you send it away? Where are Rose and Amaranth?"

"Gwynedd, it doesn't matter."

"It does matter!"

Gwynedd stared out from the cliff, and the clouds burst, releasing a deluge of water into the sky. Down in the valley, the rivers bulged against their banks, the current running swift and strong. She could see the humans, panicked and screaming, squalling like children as scrambled for shelter.

She drew her knife out of her robes and turned to face Bronwyn. "It will never be over," she said. "I will hunt the Foxglove to the end of the earth. My magic will find it, no matter where you have hidden it."

"It won't matter, Gwynedd. The Foxglove is in the human world now. Carried away by the storm. You will never find it, and even if you could, only its power can open the barriers between the worlds. It is out of your reach."

Rage boiled in Gywnedd's chest. Above, the thunder rolled, rumbling its own anger in response. "No!" Gwynedd snarled, grabbing Bronwyn by the shoulders. "How could you? How could you do this?"

"I had to stop you," Bronwyn replied. "I'm sorry, old friend, but this has gone too far. You've lost your way."

Gwynedd flung her to the stony ground. "How dare you call me your friend?!" she said. "You ... you have condemned our entire civilization!"

Bronwyn stood up, drawing her sword. "Better here than under your control. Think of Lily. Think of the refugees. What good can come from that? You aren't ready for the power of the Foxglove, Gwynedd. None of us are."

"That's not true!"

"One day, perhaps, we will be. I have seen it. The Foxglove will return, but by then, this world will have changed, and you and I will be long dead."

Gwynedd screamed, lunging forward with her knife. Bronwyn brought her sword up and parried away the strike, flinching as she used her shoulder. Gwynedd drove into her and they rolled onto the ground.

"Stop it!" Bronwyn shouted, grabbing Gwynedd's wrist.

Gwynedd hissed a breath in through clenched teeth as her friend gripped her hand, twisting it until the pain shot up her arm. Crying out, Gwynedd dropped her knife. Bronwyn stood up and kicked it away, standing over her, sword point set against her throat.

"This ... is done," she said, panting for breath. "You have to sto—"

The point of an arrow burst through her chest. Bronwyn's sentence staggered to a halting grunt, and she stared down. "Gwynedd?" she said, her voice becoming faint. "I'm … I'm … "

She wobbled on her feet and fell.

Gwynedd's eyes went wide as her friend collapsed. "Bronwyn!"

Ranke and her guards charged up the hill as Gwynedd threw herself down beside Bronwyn.

"Gwynedd!" Bronwyn gasped, coughing up a spatter of blood. "Gwynedd, I'm sorry. I didn't mean it. I'm sorry."

Her skin turned pale. Gwynedd's chest tightened. Her heart staggered as the rage fled from her mind, and she frantically searched her robes for any potion that might be used to heal, but there were none. She'd left them in the basement. Her hands flew to Bronwyn's chest as blood welled up through her fingers, flowing out onto her cloak.

"Bronwyn, I can't stop it. You have to hold on!"

Her friend reached up to touch her face, leaving a smudge of blood on Gwynedd's cheek. "I should have been there for you," she said.

Hot tears burned in Gwynedd's eyes.

"I'm sorry," Bronwyn whispered as her voice began to fail. The strength in her muscles fell away, and she sagged in Gwynedd's arms.

"For what?" Gwynedd said, holding her.

"I didn't mean to leave you … alone."

Bronwyn's eyes fluttered shut, and she lay still.

"Bronwyn?" Gwynedd called, and waited. She shook her. "Bronwyn?!"

Her body began to quake as her hands fell to her sides, and her friend's body slipped onto the ground.

Ranke came to stand over her. "This is it," she said. "The end of the rebels. Did you get what you were looking for?"

Gwynedd pressed herself up, staggering. "No," she answered. "It was too late."

"I'm sorry to hear that," Ranke said. "But whatever trinket she stole from you can't be worth more than I can give. In a matter of days, I will have rounded up this woman's followers, and it will be over."

The rebels, Gwynedd thought. *Small power over a small world. Was that all her friend's life was worth?*

Gwynedd wiped her face with her forearm. "She was worth more than you will ever know."

Ranke sneered. "And yet she died for nothing."

Gwynedd turned slowly around. Anger and resentment like she'd never felt before filled her eyes, and in her heart, a hatred rose up, with a breath so cold … it burned.

"Well," she said, lifting a hand to the sky. "We can't have that."

A bolt of lightning emerged from the clouds and crashed down upon Ranke. She shrieked as all the rage and fury of the storm poured out of Gwynedd's heart and split the woman in two.

Her guards staggered back, terrified as they cowered against the earth.

Gwynedd walked past them. "Release the people of Hane," she said. "Or I will come back for you."

They nodded, begging and pleading for their lives as she continued on. There was work to do. Her people would survive without her help, though perhaps only in some base fashion, and in the end, it would not matter. Bronwyn said it herself. One day, the Foxglove would return.

Gwynedd knelt down and picked up her knife.

And on that day, she would be ready.

From the Author

I hope you enjoyed reading Queens of Iris as much as I loved writing it. If you don't mind me asking you for a favor, please consider leaving a review. I read them all, and each one goes a long way towards helping a book succeed. Thank you.

Sincerely,
Aaron McQueen

Also Available from Aaron McQueen

Special Thanks to my Patreon Subscribers!

Theresa Uber

Timothy Tortal

Matthew Edmondson

Made in the USA
Monee, IL
12 February 2020